Race took her by both shoulders

"You are the most infuriating female! Every time I try to do something nice for you, I get kicked in the teeth!"

Lorinda began to laugh.

"What's so damned funny?" he demanded.

"The idea of m-me k-kicking you in the t-teeth," she gasped through her laughter.

"Oh, so you think it's funny, do you? Well, see what you think of this!"

Before she realized what he meant to do, he had drawn her against him and brought his mouth down hard over hers. She had seen him kiss his leading ladies on the screen and had shivered with vicarious delight, but nothing could have prepared her for the reality. A heady tingling sensation began at the back of her neck and continued through her body as his mouth plundered hers.

All common sense told her she should end this, but her body had ideas of its own....

WELCOME
TO THE WONDERFUL WORLD
OF *Harlequin Romances*

Interesting, informative and entertaining,
each Harlequin Romance portrays an appealing
and original love story. With a varied array
of settings, we may lure you on an African safari,
to a quaint Welsh village, or an exotic Riviera
location—anywhere and everywhere that adventurous
men and women fall in love.

As publishers of Harlequin Romances, we're
extremely proud of our books. Since 1949,
Harlequin Enterprises has built its publishing
reputation on the solid base of quality and
originality. Our stories are the most popular
paperback romances sold in North America; every
month, six new titles are released and sold at
nearly every book-selling store in Canada and the
United States.

A free catalog listing all Harlequin Romances
can be yours by writing to the

HARLEQUIN READER SERVICE,
(In the U.S.) 2504 West Southern Avenue, Tempe, AZ 85282
(In Canada) Stratford, Ontario, N5A 6W2

We sincerely hope you enjoy reading
this Harlequin Romance.

Yours truly,

THE PUBLISHERS
Harlequin Romances

The Tall Dark Stranger

Valerie Parv

Harlequin Books

TORONTO • NEW YORK • LONDON
AMSTERDAM • PARIS • SYDNEY • HAMBURG
STOCKHOLM • ATHENS • TOKYO • MILAN

Original hardcover edition published in 1983
by Mills & Boon Limited

ISBN 0-373-02589-0

Harlequin Romance first edition December 1983

CHAPTER ONE

THE first prediction came true on Monday night.

With her usual effortless grace, Lorinda Fleming bounced up the three flights of stairs to the small flat she shared with her mother, pausing only long enough to pull a sheaf of letters out of their box and thrust them into her handbag. She came up short as she caught sight of a figure standing at the head of the stairs.

'Mrs Clarke! You gave me a fright standing there.'

'Oh, Miss Fleming, I didn't want to risk missing you, and you'd already left your office when I called, so I've been standing here waiting since . . . since . . .' The elderly woman's voice broke on a sob.

'Since what? Please Mrs Clarke, tell me what's happened!'

The neighbour pulled herself together with an obvious effort. 'It's your poor mother, dear. She's had a heart attack.'

Fear clutched at Lorinda's throat. 'Heart attack? Oh, dear God, she's not . . .'

'She's alive and the doctor said she's not in danger,' Mrs Clarke interposed quickly, seeing Lorinda's face drain of colour. 'But they had to take her to the hospital, you see.'

'I must go to her at once. Which hospital?'

'St Clare's. You're to ask for Dr Maddison when you get there.'

Her thoughts racing, Lorinda started back down the stairs, but turned for a moment and smiled at her neighbour. 'Thanks, Mrs Clarke, for waiting to tell me.'

'That's all right, dear. Give your mother my love.'

The words 'mother' and 'love' echoed in her ears as she climbed back into the battered red Mini she used to travel to work. Her mother was all she had in the world. If anything happened to her . . .

With a jolt she realised she was steering straight towards a telegraph pole, so she pushed such distressing thoughts from her mind and concentrated on the mechanical task of guiding the little car through the evening traffic to the hospital.

At St Clare's she quickly located Dr Maddison, who confirmed what Mrs Clarke had told her. Arna Fleming had suffered a heart attack but was out of danger and resting comfortably. The doctor wanted to keep her in hospital for a short time for observation and tests, and Lorinda agreed at once.

Now, as she stood at her mother's bedside gazing down at the pale, still form, a lump rose to her throat. 'Please be all right,' she implored softly.

At the slight sound her mother stirred and her eyelids fluttered open, then her hand groped for Lorinda's and clasped it. 'Hello, darling.'

The lump grew until it threatened to choke her. 'Hello, Mum—don't talk now, you're supposed to be resting.'

'Nonsense. It was just a bit of indigestion, nothing I haven't had before.'

'You mean you've felt ill before and said nothing? Oh, Mum, you might have prevented this if you'd said something!'

She should have known it was useless. The last person Arna Fleming ever worried about was herself. It had been like that ever since Lorinda could remember. First, she had sacrificed her dream of a settled home to follow the whims of her entertainer husband. When he finally tired of them both, she had taken over Lorinda's upbringing and worked long hours as a secretary to ensure they were adequately fed and clothed and to send Lorinda to a good school.

Gradually her mother's hold slackened and she drifted off to sleep, which, the nurse assured Lorinda, was a good sign. Nevertheless, she decided to sit awhile at her mother's bedside. Although visiting hours were over, the nurse winked conspiratorially and made a show of turning her back. Gratefully, Lorinda sank into the only chair and studied the still figure in the bed.

Yes, it was typical of her mother to ignore the symptoms of illness. Even before Lorinda's father left them, she had had to be the strong one, making family decisions, budgeting carefully to balance his excesses and looking the other way while he conducted his affairs with the young showgirls who eagerly offered him their favours in exchange for career advantages. As a child, Lorinda had been in awe of her father, the debonair singer and dancer, Rick Brennan. Now, at twenty-three, she was old enough to understand that he had never been happy as a family man. She and Arna had been whims to him, to be cast aside as soon as they became encumbrances. Rick had never even allowed her to call him Daddy, preferring her to use his first name which did not remind him so much that he, too, was growing older. Heaven knew how he would have reacted if she had made him a grandfather, as well she could have done by now if the right man had come along.

She sighed deeply. There was not much chance of either—the right man, or making Rick a grandfather, she told herself. The years of watching her mother suffer had convinced her that marriage was not for her. Besides which, Rick had dropped out of sight some years ago, so if she did ever have a child, he would probably never know he was a grandfather. Even if he knew his wife was in hospital he would not come rushing to her side. Illness was abhorrent to him because he inevitably associated it with age and decay.

Deliberately Lorinda channelled her thoughts away from the troubled past, thinking instead about her work which was the mainstay of her life. But this path had hazards of its own, for it reminded her of today's lunchtime visit to the gypsy fortune-teller at the shopping complex near her office, and she preferred not to think about that after tonight's uncanny coincidence.

For it *was* just coincidence, she told herself firmly. She hadn't wanted to visit the gypsy in the first place, but Marla, the secretary-receptionist at Metropolitan Casting and her best friend, had insisted it would be fun, so reluctantly she had gone along.

They found the gypsy in a garishly striped tent set up in one of the shopping centre courtyards. 'Cross my palm with silver,' the woman inside had ordered.

Marla looked at Lorinda and giggled, but they were silenced by a sharp look from the woman. 'Do not mock what you do not understand,' she commanded.

Subdued, Marla placed a silver coin in the woman's grimy hand and was rewarded with a list of predictions which, if even half of them were true, would ensure her fame, fortune and the longest of lives.

When it was Lorinda's turn, she placed a coin in the woman's hand and took her place across the table, expecting to hear much the same as Marla had. However, as soon as she took Lorinda's hand, the woman stiffened and gripped it convulsively.

In spite of herself, Lorinda was alarmed. 'What is it? What do you see?'

'Hush! You have a most unusual hand. I see . . . a

great deal of courage and self-reliance. The signs say you were deserted while very young.'

Lorinda jumped, not realising that her small movement confirmed the gypsy's guess and encouraged her to follow this line of reasoning while she covertly watched Lorinda herself for more clues. After a little more about her past, she began to reveal Lorinda's future.

'I see three things for you,' she intoned, 'the first is that very soon, someone close to you will fall seriously ill. But you must not worry—that person's time is not yet. The second thing is that you will receive a large sum of money from an unexpected source.'

Relieved to be back on the plane of makebelieve again, Lorinda almost laughed aloud as she thought how unlikely *that* prediction was to come true. Still, she could not resist asking, 'And the third thing?'

The woman's dark eyes bored into her and seemed to draw her forward until their heads were close together over the baize-covered table. 'You will meet a tall dark stranger who will take from you something you value.'

Almost choking with the effort of holding back their laughter, Lorinda and Marla supported one another out of the tent into the reassuring brightness of the modern shopping centre. 'For heaven's sake!' spluttered Lorinda when they were safely out of the gypsy's earshot. 'A tall dark stranger! How corny can you get?'

'But admit it,' Marla challenged her, 'you were really fooled for a while. That bit about someone close to you falling ill was spooky.'

'But she ruined the effect by saying I was going to come into money,' Lorinda smiled. 'Who in the world would be leaving *me* any money? I don't have any relatives at all, far less old and wealthy ones.'

Marla nodded sympathetically. 'Unfortunately,

neither do I.' She glanced at her watch. 'And even though she predicted a rosy future for me, I won't have *any* sort of future if I'm late back from lunch again!'

The two quickened their steps, to arrive at work just as the Town Hall clock began to chime the hour. Lorinda was not as concerned as Marla about getting back exactly on time. As a trainee agent with Max Rowley's agency, she often worked long hours, so had an understanding with Max that she could take other time off to compensate when the workload permitted. Not for the first time, she considered how lucky she was to have found her vocation so easily. Max Rowley had been her father's agent until he went away and was a good friend of the family. He had been glad to give Lorinda her break, although she knew he could not have afforded to keep her on if she hadn't shown a real aptitude for the work. She was surprised to find that showbusiness appealed to her at all, given her background, but found she had a talent and liking for matching the right performer to a job. Since Max was also an agent for a number of actors and visiting artists from overseas, she also had the chance to work in the glamorous but demanding world of show business management.

Her mother stirred and moaned in her sleep and Lorinda came back to her surroundings with a start. She half rose from the chair to glance at the monitor over the bed, but it showed no change in the steady rhythm of Arna's heart, so she subsided again, aware that her own heart was the one that was racing.

She groped in her handbag for a handkerchief to wipe away the beads of perspiration which had sprung up on her forehead and her hand encountered the bundle of letters she had thrust into her bag just before she met Mrs Clarke on the stairs.

To distract herself, she thumbed through the pile. Most of the letters were bills—telephone, which was an extravagance but necessary for her work, electricity, dentist—distastefully, she pushed them back into her bag. There would be time enough to worry about them later. The last letter was in a slim buff-coloured envelope with the name Mackenzie-Hill-Greenwood stamped in elegant raised type along the bottom. Lorinda couldn't recall anyone by any of those names. Perhaps it was something to do with work, sent to her home address by mistake. Then she realised how foolish it was to sit speculating when the simple act of opening the letter would answer all her questions. Yet for some reason, she was afraid to.

Resolutely she slid a thumbnail along the top of the envelope and pulled out a single sheet of buff-coloured paper bearing the same motif as the envelope. Her heart skipped another beat as she saw the salutation on the letter. It said 'Dear Miss Brennan'—but who could be writing to her under her father's name? She and her mother had been using Arna's maiden name ever since Rick left. Confused, she scanned the typed paragraphs, and drew a deep breath of astonishment as she assimilated the contents.

The letter was signed by a Mr Andrew Hill who introduced himself as a partner in a firm of solicitors. He was acting, he wrote, on behalf of Miss Janet Ryland who had passed away recently and provided for Lorinda to receive a sum of money from her estate.

Miss Janet Ryland—dreamily, she stared into space, her eyes clouding with tears as she thought of the grandmotherly woman who had nursed her for two years as a small child. Dear Janey! It had been another of Rick Brennan's whims that his little daughter have a nurse so he and Arna would be free to pursue their social life and keep the odd hours performers' lives demanded. Arna had never wanted anyone to take charge of her child, but had given in as soon as she met Janet Ryland. All Lorinda could remember of her from those days was a warm, loving nature and the largest lap in the world, as well as a unique ability to change voices when reading fairytales aloud. She remembered how deliciously scared she had been when Janey played the part of the wicked witch or pitched her voice high and bell-like as the good fairy. That period when they had lived in the same house for two whole years running, and Janey was always there even when her parents were away on tour, had been the happiest of Lorinda's life.

Inevitably, they moved house again when Rick accepted an engagement as M.C. at a theatre restaurant, and Janey had been unable to leave her home to go with the family. Lorinda never forgot the wrench of that parting, brutal enough for her to resolve never to risk loving anyone ever again. Although she had been very young, she had kept that promise, she thought wryly, never wholly giving her affection to anyone except her mother. Not even a dog or a cat had been allowed to claim her heart, for she remembered only too well the pain of parting.

She and Janey had kept in touch ever since as Lorinda's letters grew from childish scribble through chatty teenage missives to adult correspondence. But Janey's eyesight failed eventually, and finally a friend wrote to say although she would not be able to send any more letters herself, she hoped Lorinda would keep writing to her. This, Lorinda had done faithfully. Her last letter had been posted only three weeks ago. Occasionally, someone from the nursing home where Janey spent her last years would write to say how much the old lady enjoyed receiving the letters and having them read to her.

Now Janey was gone. Once again, Lorinda felt a heart-wrenching sense of desolation at this, the most final of partings. She had never risked visiting the elderly nurse or allowed herself to think of the correspondence with Janey as an expression of love, but now she knew it had been, and the news of her death came as a bitter blow.

Through a veil of tears she finished reading the letter, and the amount which had been bequeathed to her made her gasp in astonishment—six thousand dollars! She had always thought of Janey as being like herself, not poverty-stricken, but having to budget with care. The bequest came as a total surprise.

Then another thought turned her blood to ice. 'You will receive a large sum of money from an unexpected source.'

Six thousand dollars was a large sum of money and Janet Ryland was certainly an unexpected source. But how could the gypsy have known?

Lorinda began to feel a little faint as she considered the implications. Somehow the gypsy had known that her mother was going to fall ill? Thank goodness she had also said, 'That person's time is not yet'. Then there was the sum of money . . . which left only the third prediction, that she would meet a tall dark stranger who would take from her something she valued.

A great shudder racked her slender body. She had been so sure that the trite predictions were nonsense. In desperation, she tried to cling to the thought that it might be coincidence. No one could see into the future. Yet she was forced to face the fact that two of the predictions had already come shockingly true. Could she afford to dismiss the third quite so readily?

Next morning when she walked into the office, Max

Rowley looked at her in surprise. 'I didn't expect to see you here today, Lori. How is Arna?'

'She's much better, thanks. The doctor was pleased that she had a comfortable night. I was with her until quite late and she slept most of the time. They're keeping her for a few days for some tests.'

'Would I be able to visit her later today?'

'She'd love to see you,' she said warmly. 'But you mustn't take her anything to eat or drink. They've put her on a special diet.'

'I'll remember that. And if you need any time off to visit her, just take it. Don't even bother to ask, okay?'

Her eyes met his in silent understanding. Max had been more like a father to her than Rick had ever been, but she was always careful never to abuse the advantage it gave her. 'Thanks, Max, I appreciate that.'

He patted her hand then disappeared into his own office. When his door closed, Marla came hurrying across the room. 'Max told me about your mother. Is she all right?'

'The doctor says she'll be fine, if she can be persuaded to take things easy for a while. But you know my mother.'

Marla nodded. She had visited the Flemings' flat often enough to know what a tireless worker Arna was and how difficult it would be to persuade her to rest. 'If there's anything I can do—cover for you here while you visit her . . . just name it.'

'Thanks, Marla. I'll let you know if there's anything.'

The other girl turned back towards her own desk but before she could move, Lorinda caught her arm. 'Marla?'

'Yes, what is it?'

'About that gypsy we visited yesterday . . .'

'You're not still thinking about her, are you? It was

fun, but don't take it seriously.'

Lorinda bit her lower lip thoughtfully. 'That's what I thought yesterday, until ... well, she *did* say my mother was going to be ill.'

Marla's eyes widened, then she broke into a broad grin. 'She didn't say your mother, just someone close to you. Coincidence, that's all.'

'I thought so, too, until her second prediction came true,' said Lorinda.

'Oh, Lori! What happened?'

As briefly as she could, Lorinda told her the story of her old nurse. Marla whistled when she mentioned the amount she was to receive.

'Six thousand, huh? That is quite a large sum of money, especially to us working girls. But I see what you mean about the gypsy—she is getting a bit too close for comfort, isn't she?'

'And there's still the third prediction, remember.'

'Well, there's only one thing for you to do,' announced Marla.

'And what's that?'

'Keep clear of tall dark strangers from now on!'

Given the number of men in Lorinda's life—or the lack of them—she considered this should be fairly easy advice to follow. She had, however, reckoned without the arrival of Max Rowley's newest client.

'What time is *he* due to arrive?' Marla asked her just before lunchtime.

'If you mean Race Wolfendale, I should say any time. Max met him at the airport early this morning and took him to his hotel to unwind. He said he'd drop by later, when he's slept off his jet-lag, I suppose.'

Marla stared at her in amazement. 'How can you take this so calmly? I'm dying to meet Mr Smooth himself!'

Lorinda glanced anxiously across the room, but the door to Max's office was still closed. 'Better not let the boss hear you use that expression,' she cautioned. 'I don't know where the press got such a label from!'

Marla laughed. 'One look at him and you can see where they get it from. He has a voice like crême de cacao and when he acts, it's as if there isn't another actor in the film. He's won two Oscars, you know.'

'Saints preserve us, a fan!' groaned Lorinda. 'Just don't swoon all over the place when he walks in. We're supposed to impress him as professionals.'

'I shall be Miss Cool to his Mr Smooth—watch me,' promised Marla as she returned to her own desk.

Observing the young receptionist as she worked, Lorinda doubted that very much. She jumped a foot every time anyone came through the door and spent much more time than usual fussing with her hair and make-up. Luckily, *she* wasn't disturbed by the imminent arrival of Race Wolfendale, Lorinda thought. Since joining the agency, she had worked with enough stars not to be affected by them. After all, they were still just people.

But her resolve was shaken to its core when Race Wolfendale finally walked into the office. Unlike many of the stars she had worked with, who looked disappointingly ordinary in real life, he looked every inch a star. Granted, his clothes were simple enough, although obviously expensive—a chocolate knit shirt teamed with beige figure-hugging pants tucked into cowboy boots. It was more the overwhelming presence of the man which seemed to precede him into the room. Although she had prepared a backgrounder on him for release to the media and knew most of his personal data, nothing had prepared her for the sheer dynamism he exuded. He was well over six feet tall with such a superb physique that she decided he must spend every waking hour in the gym.

When at last she worked up the courage to look him in the eye, she flinched at the naked power she saw reflected there. It was like staring into the sun, because his eyes were like burning coals, set deep into shadowed sockets, giving him a devilish air which she was sure contributed to his box office success. His hair was very thick and waving, jet black with the merest trace of grey at the temples, although whether this was the handiwork of nature or an expert Hollywood hairdresser, she wasn't sure.

Lorinda rose automatically as he came in. Now she became aware that she was clutching the edge of her desk to steady herself. With a tremendous effort she wrenched herself away from those compelling eyes and fixed her gaze on the top button of his shirt, left casually open so that tendrils of coal black hair curled provocatively around the shirt neckline. At least that sight was marginally less disturbing than facing those all-knowing eyes.

'G-good morning, Mr Wolfendale, w-welcome to Australia,' she stammered, sure that she sounded as gauche as the teenagers who waited outside his stage door. If he noticed her confusion, he ignored it.

'Good morning, ma'am, and thank you. You must be Miss Fleming.'

'That's right, Max Rowley's assistant.'

'He told me. Is he in?'

As if on cue, Max's door flew open and the agent strode across the room to welcome his new client. They exchanged pleasantries, then Max escorted Race Wolfendale into his own office and closed the door.

At once Lorinda sagged against her desk.

'There, didn't I tell you he was something?' Marla

purred. 'You look as if you've been hit by a thunderbolt, and you told *me* to act cool!'

'I do nothing of the sort, ' Lorinda protested hotly, feeling her face colour embarrassingly. 'It was just . . . he . . .'

'You were knocked out by him—admit it,' Marla teased. 'It's nothing to be ashamed of. After all, half the females around this planet feel the same way, and that's just the effect of seeing him on the big screen. We're in the same office with him!'

'You're imagining things,' she snapped at Marla, aware that she was being unfair but unable to stop herself. 'I'm just tired, that's all. I was up very late last night.'

Quickly she picked up her handbag and escaped to the ladies' room, where she splashed cool water over her fevered face. It *was* the unaccustomed late night and the worry about her mother, she assured herself. Still, the image of those burning eyes stayed with her, and the honeyed tone of his voice haunted her as she went about the routine of repairing her make-up and thrusting a brush through her thick mane.

The face which stared back at her from the mirror did look feverish, with telltale splashes of red staining her high cheekbones and standing out against her skin, which was the colour of coffee well laced with cream, the result of her easy ability to tan without burning. Her hair was her best feature, she mused irrelevantly, as she drew the brush through it. Despite an almost weekly resolution to have it cut short, she enjoyed the feel of it swishing around her shoulders. It was the colour of cornsilk shot through with lighter highlights which other girls accused her of having professionally streaked. Luckily, that had never been necessary—the combination of nature's gifts and regular exposure to sunlight had done the job for her.

Now she let the rhythmic brushing soothe her as it always did. One hundred strokes every night before bedtime had become as much a part of her day as breathing and the activity had become a kind of substitute meditation. Already she felt much calmer and able to think about the last few minutes objectively.

It wasn't as if anything had *happened*, after all. The man had simply walked in, said good morning and asked to see Max. So why did she have this heady sensation, as if he had swept her off her feet and carried her into Max's private office?

For heaven's sake! Marla must be getting to her with her silly gossip about Race Wolfendale's impact on women. She, of all people, should be immune to such obvious theatrics.

If only he hadn't been tall and dark and a stranger. She paused in mid-brushstroke. Now where had that idea come from? She had already made up her mind to forget all about the gypsy's silly prediction. Besides, Race Wolfendale was a client, here to star at the opening of a luxurious new Barrier Reef island resort. After a few days in Sydney, he would fly north and that would be the last she would see of him. Max had said he might go with Race to see that all went well with the opening, but after that, most of their professional obligations to him would be over.

Feeling considerably better, she stepped out into the corridor, only to collide with the object of her thoughts. An unaccountable thrill ran through her as Race Wolfendale reached out a hand to steady her, bringing her hard up against him.

'Whoa there! They should put traffic lights on this corner!'

She tried to ignore the disturbingly masculine feel of him pressing against her in the narrow corridor.

'I'm sorry, I wasn't looking where I was going. But you're right, this corner could use some sort of signal.'

She was babbling and she knew it, but she seemed fated to lose all self-control in the face of this extraordinary man. The fact that, having steadied her, he still held her in his powerful grip only added to her confusion. Why didn't he release her and be done with it? But it seemed he had been looking for her. 'Your boss kindly gave me the green light to ask you out to lunch,' he told her.

'Well, I'm sorry, but I can't go,' she said at once, then was sorry she had been so blunt. He didn't deserve rudeness, after all.

He seemed genuinely disappointed. 'I should have checked first to see if you had another date,' he conceded. 'How about tomorrow, then?'

'No, I can't ... I mean, I go to classes in my lunch breaks.'

This was stretching the truth, but she hoped she would be forgiven for it. After all, she did go to yoga classes on two out of her five lunch breaks, tomorrow being one of them.

At once he released her and stood back to let her pass. 'I see, thanks for letting me know where I stand.'

The coldness in his tone told her he understood the situation exactly. Well, let him. He was probably so used to having every woman for miles swooning at his feet that he couldn't accept there was one who would turn him down. The lesson would probably be good for him.

Yet shortly after, as she saw him leave with Max, Lorinda couldn't help feeling a pang of disappointment. What would it have been like to accompany him to one of the excellent restaurants she knew in the area and sit across from him at an intimate table for two? They would talk, and every head would turn their way as he was recognised. It would have been fun, she thought regretfully. More than that, she would have liked to find out what he was really like under that polished Hollywood veneer. For in those fascinating eyes she had glimpsed an inner fire which both excited and challenged her.

Marla had been disappointed and Max was openly annoyed when she refused to go to lunch with Race Wolfendale. Max saw it as part of her job and couldn't understand her reluctance. The fact that her refusal had antagonised an important new client had also upset him.

How could she explain to them all, or even to herself, that she couldn't go out with Race Wolfendale because he was tall and dark and a stranger? And in spite of all the logic she summoned, she was unnerved by that ridiculous prediction.

CHAPTER TWO

'YOU'RE obviously feeling better today!'

Arna Fleming was sitting up in bed working an intricate design in needlepoint. She put the work aside and smiled as her daughter came in. 'Yes, much better, thanks. Doctor Maddison is going to let me come home in a day or so.'

Lorinda shook her head. 'Not home. You know the first thing you'd do is spring-clean everything in case a speck of dust had crept in while you were away! I've arranged for you to spend the next fortnight at a very good convalescent home in the Blue Mountains.'

A shadow crossed her mother's face. 'But, Lori, we can't afford any such thing!'

'Yes, we can,' she said firmly. 'I told you about my legacy—it's more than enough to meet the fees, with quite a bit left over.'

'But that money was meant for you!'

'There's nothing else I'd rather do with it.' Lorinda looked pleadingly at her mother. 'Please let me do this for you!'

Arna sighed, but she recognised her own streak of stubbornness in her daughter. 'All right, I accept. This bout has left me feeling rather drained. A few days in the mountains sounds heavenly.' She patted the bed alongside her. 'Now enough about me. Tell me about this famous film star you've been looking after. I was reading about him in the papers this morning.'

Lorinda perched on the side of the bed. 'That would have been about the press conference we arranged yesterday. He was a hit with all the lady journalists.'

'Sounds like you don't think very much of him,' her mother commented.

'Actually, I haven't given him much thought at all,' she countered, which was far from being the truth. She had thought about very little else since Race Wolfendale had walked into the office three days ago. Never could she remember being so affected by one person as she had been by him. The few words they had exchanged and the one moment when he steadied her against him in the corridor were indelibly imprinted on her brain.

'But what is he really like?' her mother persisted.

Lorinda pondered for a moment. 'He looks exactly like he does on screen. Even the hair is his own!'

'But is he vain, arrogant? Come on, Lori—from your reluctance to discuss him, anyone would think you'd fallen in love with him already!'

'No!' she protested vehemently. 'Don't be silly, Mum, it's nothing like that. He's a client, that's all. I'm not impressed by pop stars, movie actors and their types any more. Of course, Marla thinks the sun shines out of his eyes. "Can I get you a coffee, Mr Wolfendale?" "Would you like some more cream, Mr Wolfendale?" "Will you walk all over me, Mr Wolfendale?" '

It was such a good imitation of the young receptionist that Arna laughed, but her eyes remained serious. 'Just what is it about Race Wolfendale that has you so steamed up?' she asked quietly.

How could she tell her mother about such a stupid thing as a gypsy prediction, especially since she couldn't be sure herself if that was the explanation? Over and over, Lorinda told herself that she was only guarding herself against the slim chance that the gypsy

was right. But deep down, she knew there was more to
it than that, perhaps the fear that, if she let herself,
she could like Race Wolfendale far too much. She was
still not prepared to risk the pain of an eventual
parting to find out.

Deliberately she made her tone light and inconsequ-
ential. 'Don't worry, Mum, I'm not about to fall for
our Hollywood superstar. He's spending the next few
days holidaying on the north coast at a secret location
where the press can't find him. After that, he flies to
the Barrier Reef for the opening at Windi Bay, so I
may not even see him again.'

'I see.' Arna's hand found hers on the bedclothes.
'Lori, I know you don't want me to interfere, but I
hope, when the right man comes along, you won't let
. . . the past . . . stand in your way.'

Lorinda's laugh was forced. 'You know I always
welcome your advice, but there's nothing to worry
about. I don't plan on losing my heart to anyone just
yet, especially not to Race Wolfendale.'

Max Rowley was waiting by her desk when she
hurried into the office. A glance at her watch told her
she was only five minutes over her allotted lunch hour.
'Sorry I'm late,' she breathed.

'That's okay. I told you to take all the time you
need. How was Arna today?'

'She's doing very well, thanks. She told me you
went to see her yesterday. It meant a lot to her.'

'My pleasure. You know I think the world of your
mother. But look, you spent your lunch-break at the
hospital. I don't suppose you had time to eat?'

'Well, no, I . . .'

'I thought not, so I want you to do me a favour.
There's an old actor acquaintance of mine in my
office. I want you to take him out and buy him some
lunch.'

Lorinda's heart sank. Why did she always have to be the one to look after his waifs and strays? But Max was already peeling notes out of his wallet and there was such a look of appeal in his expression that she relented. 'All right, lead the way,' she said resignedly, and was rewarded with a look of such gratitude that she was heartened.

Max meant well, but he was always an easy target for anyone in the entertainment business who was down on his luck. He didn't seem able to say no and word got around, so there was usually at least one out-of-work performer depending on him. Occasionally Lorinda was roped in to look after one of his charges, and it looked as if today was one of those days. She squared her shoulders, fixed a professional smile on her face and followed Max into his office.

'Lorinda, this is David Hewitt. David, my assistant, Lorinda Fleming.'

'Delighted to meet you, Miss Fleming.'

Even if he had not spoken she would have tagged him as British, a one-time Shakespearean actor, she decided, judging by his courtly mannerisms and the half-bow he executed as she came in. His clothes had seen better days, but they were at least clean and well cared for, if threadbare. As her eye travelled to his cuffs she saw him selfconsciously pull the jacket sleeves down over the frayed shirtsleeves. So he still cared about what others thought—that was unusual, but promising. In her experience, when they reached the stage of accepting hand-outs, their own pride had long since vanished.

This man seemed different, somehow, and Lorinda decided it was the unfathomable quality in his expression, evident even though most of his face was hidden behind a small, full beard and bushy silver-grey sideburns and his eyes were shielded by thick rimless glasses. Behind the glasses his eyes shone diamond-bright and she felt an inexplicable surge of recognition as their eyes met. She must have seen him on a stage somewhere, she decided, and postponed further speculation. With a surge of sympathy she noticed that his hands were gnarled and arthritic, the backs spotted with dark brown marks. His shoulders were hunched over, probably with the same affliction, otherwise he would have been a remarkably tall man. Something about him made her want to like him, and she was surprised to find herself looking forward to the prospect of their lunch together.

Mindful that it was Max's money they were spending, she took him to a modest little French bistro tucked away down a side street near the office. Since it was probably the only decent meal David Hewitt would get all day, she ordered three generous courses for him and chose an omelette and French salad for herself. She could have sworn that his eyes twinkled with amusement when she placed the order, but she decided she was imagining things.

'Now, Mr Hewitt,' she said when the waiter had gone, 'tell me about yourself.'

'Before I launch into the dreary story of my life, could I possibly persuade you to call me David?'

Smiling, she agreed, and insisted that he call her Lorinda. Hesitantly at first, then with increasing assurance, he told her how he had started his career as an assistant stage manager with a repertory company in England, doing the dogsbody jobs which eventually led to small walk-on parts and, gradually, to better roles. She had been right about his Shakespearean background, she discovered, because he then went on to tour as a principal with a small Stratford company.

'But if you were doing so well, then how . . .' She

hesitated, not sure how much one lunch gave her the right to pry.

'How did I end up like this? It's a long story,' he admitted sadly. 'The bottle probably had something to do with it. Then there was a woman . . .' He tailed off.

Impulsively she covered his hand with her own. 'Don't talk about it if you'd rather not.'

He gave her a grateful smile which did very strange things to her insides. 'I knew you'd understand. Max was right, you are a very special person.'

She felt warm colour suffusing her cheeks and was thankful for the restaurant's dim lighting. 'Max is prejudiced,' she said lightly.

David Hewitt toasted her with his glass of iced water. 'Maybe. But if so, then I am too.'

As they parted at the entrance to her office building, he caught her hand and lifted it to his lips. 'Thank you for an enchanting experience, my dear Lorinda.' Then he surprised her by asking if he might see her again. To her own astonishment, she heard herself agreeing and wondered why on earth she should feel so attracted to an ageing, down-and-out former actor. They arranged to attend a free outdoor music recital being staged by the city council. At least she didn't have to worry about how he could afford to entertain her, she thought wryly as she returned to her desk.

Max was delighted when she told him how much she had enjoyed David's company, but raised an eyebrow in surprise when he heard that she was planning to see the man again soon. 'Do you think that's wise? After all, you don't know very much about him.'

'You were anxious enough for me to take him to lunch. Are you afraid he might carry me off?'

'No, of course not,' Max responded gruffly. 'I just don't want you getting hurt, that's all.'

How she could possibly get hurt by someone as
sweet and harmless as David Hewitt, she couldn't
imagine, so she dismissed Max's odd behaviour from
her mind. He was acting very strangely altogether at
the moment, but she put that down to the stress of
looking after an important client like Race Wolfendale.
Even though the star was vacationing incognito on the
north coast, it was still a strain. There was the media
to deal with and the arrangements for the Windi Bay
opening so even without the star himself, they were
ever mindful of his presence in the country because of
the sheer volume of work which went with organising
his tour.

So the outdoor concert she attended with David
Hewitt came as a welcome relief in the middle of a
hectic few days. Entitled 'Mod to Mozart', it was an
orchestral smörgasbörd of modern and classical music,
well chosen and skilfully executed in an enchanting
setting beside Sydney Harbour.

During the intermission, Lorinda stretched her long
legs out in front of her and luxuriated in the feel of the
grass brushing her skin. 'I'm so glad we came,' she
sighed.

David poured them each a cup of black coffee from
the vacuum flask she had brought and passed her one.
'Don't you wish I'd been able to take you to a fancy
restaurant or a new show?'

'Don't be silly! It's a heavenly evening, the music is
superb. What more could I possibly want?'

He rolled over on the grass and propped his head up
on one elbow so he could look at her. 'I think you
honestly mean that. You *are* happy with simple
pleasures, aren't you, Lorinda?'

'That's right. You could say I had enough of the
bright lights while I was growing up to realise that
there are more important things in life.'

'Such as?'

Without quite knowing why, she found herself telling him all about her quixotic father and the gypsy life she led as a child, which made her long for security and stability now. There was something about this softly spoken English actor which made her want to confide in him, as she had never been able to do with anyone other than her mother before.

Suddenly she realised she was doing all the talking. 'That's enough about me. I didn't mean to bore you with my life history.'

Gently he placed his hand over hers on the grass, exerting the lightest pressure so she could feel the warmth of his skin on hers. 'Poor Lorinda,' he mused, 'it wasn't what you'd call an ideal childhood, was it?'

'But it wasn't all bad,' she said hastily. 'We always had somewhere to live and enough to eat. Lots of families don't even have that.'

'But they have the security of a loving family around them, and that's what you missed the most—wasn't it?'

'I suppose so.'

His tone became serious. 'One thing, Lorinda, try not to let your mother's experience prevent you from having a fulfilling relationship of your own. It could work out quite differently, you know, with the right man.'

'On the other hand, it could work out the same, something I'm just not prepared to risk,' she said, injecting a note of finality into her voice. Despite his age and infirmities, she liked David Hewitt more than any man she had ever met, and that was all the more reason to ensure he didn't get too close to her.

After the concert they strolled along the Harbour foreshore, watching the lights of passing ships twinkle like jewels on the wine-dark sea. Below them, the

Opera House looked like a great many-masted schooner with all its sails aloft and billowing in a phantom wind. Somewhere along their walk, David had tucked her arm into his, but it was so comfortable that she didn't object. Rather, she found herself enjoying the cosiness of the arm-in-arm stroll, while David conjured up theatrical quotations to match various moments.

However, she had to suppress a shiver of mixed concern and excitement when they reached a stone wall separating the parkland from the Harbour waters. Here, David turned to her as he rested against the low wall. In the half-dark, he seemed changed, the angles and planes of his face smoothing out so she could glimpse the handsome man he must once have been. He reminded her of someone, but she couldn't pinpoint who it was. The feeling teased at her until she pushed it aside in annoyance. It would come to her sooner or later.

Leaning this way against the wall, he lost some of the ungainly stoop and she found herself wishing he could straighten to his full height, forgetting that, of course, he couldn't.

She could hardly believe her ears when he began to recite softly, ' "Doubt that the stars are fire, Doubt that the sun doth move, Doubt truth to be a liar; But never doubt I love." '

A shiver ran down her spine and it was an effort to exclude the tremor from her voice. '*Hamlet*, isn't it?'

In the failing light she felt rather than saw his answering nod. 'That's right—a very moving verse, don't you think? The Bard must have had a night such as this in mind when he wrote those lines.'

For a moment Lorinda had foolishly imagined he might be directing the verse to her, but it was simply the night and the stars which had moved him to poetry. What on earth had Race Wolfendale done to her to start her seeing romance around every corner? She felt an urgent need to move, to break the disturbing spell. 'I have an idea, David. How would you like a genuine home-cooked meal?'

'Cooked at your place?'

'Best restaurant in town! My car's still parked outside the office. If you don't mind the walk back to it, we can be home ten minutes after that.'

'Done!' He took her arm again and they headed across the grass back towards the city centre. All the while, Lorinda told herself she must be crazy to invite a virtual stranger back to her flat. Granted, he was an acquaintance of Max's, but what else did she know about him except what he had told her, and that was little enough. Still, he had some endearing qualities which she found almost irresistible. He was charming, certainly, and for all his present run of bad fortune, he was educated and intelligent, so he was almost easier to talk to than she cared for. She couldn't remember the last time she had really talked about herself to anyone, least of all to a man.

When they reached her car, the lights were still burning in her office, indicating that Max was working late. David glanced up at the lighted window, then back to her. 'Er—Lorinda, would you mind if I just popped up to say hello to Max?'

She arched an eyebrow in surprise, then a thought occurred to her. 'David,' she ventured gently, 'if it's money you need . . .'

'No, it's not that. It's . . . personal. Do you mind?'

'No, of course not. I'll wait for you in the car.'

'Splendid. I shan't be long.'

He disappeared into the building and she settled herself in the driver's seat of her Mini to wait for him, noting with wry amusement that he was going to have a tight squeeze to fit his long legs into the front seat of her tiny car.

While they were sitting on the grass together earlier, she had noted then just how long his legs were, and observed that it was the second time she had come across a build like his.

An idea struck her with the force of a thunderbolt. The second time? No, it couldn't be. Or could it? Closing her eyes, she mentally superimposed the features of David Hewitt over those of Race Wolfendale. Without the beard, sideburns and glasses it was just possible—and it would certainly explain the nagging sense of familiarity she had been experiencing ever since she met David.

Since it was a night for quoting poetry, let him try 'The Assyrian came down like a wolf on the fold,' she thought furiously as she jumped from the car and slammed the door behind her. Right now, she knew just how those Assyrians felt!

Without waiting for the ageing elevator, she took the stairs two at a time and moved soundlessly into the darkened outer office. Two figures were silhouetted against the glass-panelled walls of Max's office and their voices could be heard quite distinctly through the quiet suite.

'Enough's enough, Race. I told you I wouldn't stand by and see Lori get hurt.'

Then the honeyed Californian tones, unhindered this time by the phoney British accent he had been using, 'Hell, Max, nobody's getting hurt. If anything, I'm doing the girl a favour. Thanks to that ne'er-do-well father of hers, she's a bundle of complexes.'

'Listen, Race, you're no psychologist.'

'I'm no Bluebeard either. I . . .'

Lorinda didn't want to hear any more. With bitter tears misting her eyes, she whirled towards the outer door. In her haste to escape from her sense of betrayal she didn't see the dictaphone cord stretched between her desk and Marla's, and her foot caught in it, pulling her full length on to the carpet.

'What in blazes . . .!' The door to Max's office was flung wide and yellow light spilled from it, revealing her undignified pose.

Choking on a sob, she pulled herself upright and fled down the stairs, not pausing until she reached the sanctuary of her car. With little regard for the engine, she slammed the car into gear and was pulling out from the kerb by the time Race emerged from the building with Max on his heels.

'Lorinda, stop!'

Not for anything would she halt in her headlong flight. At the risk of a speeding ticket, she swung the car around the nearest corner, setting the tyres screeching, and didn't lift her foot from the accelerator until she was several blocks away. Only then did she slow the Mini to a safer speed and allow herself to think while she negotiated the remaining distance to her home.

All along, she had been troubled by 'David Hewitt' of the quaint British manners and hangdog look. She should have woken up as soon as she confronted those dark, devilish eyes. If he had removed his pebble glasses just once . . . but he hadn't, and had allowed her to think he was an out-of-work actor who only wanted her companionship, when all along . . .

Tears began to stream down her cheeks as she recalled that Max was in on the whole wicked scheme. Max who had always been like a father to her. Damn, damn, damn! Wasn't there one person in this whole world she could trust? It didn't seem so, and she vowed there and then never to allow anyone, however innocent-seeming, to inveigle their way into her confidence again. It occurred to her that she had made the same vow some time ago, but this time would be different. She had incontrovertible proof of the duplicity of the male animal, and it would be a lifetime before one of them successfully laid claim to her affections again.

With Arna in hospital she had the flat to herself, and she was thankful for its solitude as she stumbled inside and slammed the door, leaning against it with the feeling of having reached safe harbour.

What on earth was she going to do now? She certainly couldn't return to work next day and face Max as if nothing had happened, knowing he had betrayed her to that . . . that Hollywood gigolo!

Her temper flared again as she recalled how Race had wormed his way into her confidence, and her cheeks burned when she considered how much of herself she had revealed to him.

In frustration, she flung her handbag on to a chair and headed for the bathroom, shedding clothes as she went until she was naked by the time she reached the shower. The cool water was balm to her troubled soul and she stood under the cascade for a long, long time, in the vain hope that the water would somehow wash away the memory of this terrible evening.

But she couldn't stay under a shower for the rest of her life. Reluctantly, she turned off the taps and reached for a towel, only then becoming aware that the doorbell was ringing steadily. She froze. If that was Race Wolfendale he could ring all night for all she cared.

The bell continued its insistent summons until her nerves were on edge again.

'Go away!' she yelled crossly.

'Not until you give me a chance to explain.'

'No!'

'Then I'll ring this damned thing all night.'

'Be my guest!'

With the bell ringing steadily in her ears, she retreated to her bedroom and hunted for something to put on. Maybe by the time she did that he would have grown tired of this childish game.

Her terry-towelling robe was the first garment to hand and she shrugged it on over her shower-dampened skin. But it seemed that Race meant to keep his word, because the bell kept up its strident ringing the whole time, until finally she could stand it no longer.

She stalked to the door and flung it wide, to find Race leaning insolently against the door frame, resting his weight against the bell-push. He had discarded the beard and glasses, but the bushy sideburns were still in place and he still wore the threadbare suit.

'Stop that!'

At once he straightened up and was inside her flat before she realised his intention. 'I didn't invite you in here,' she reminded him coldly.

He grinned. She knew she was supposed to be putty in his hands at the mere sight of that famous smile, but she hardened her heart. 'Okay, you're in. Say what you came to say and then leave, Mr Wolfendale—or is it Mr Hewitt until midnight, when you turn back into a rat?'

He winced. 'Ouch! But I guess I deserved that. It was a pretty mean trick to pull. But you wouldn't even let me get to first base with you as myself—admit it.'

Warily, she nodded. 'I admit that.'

'Mind telling me why?'

How could she tell him she had been warned off him by a gypsy fortune-teller, or more precisely, warned against tall dark strangers—and he qualified on all three counts. Despair welled up within her. 'I don't have to explain,' she countered. 'I just didn't want to go out with you. Surely it isn't the first time a woman has turned you down?'

'No,' he responded evenly. 'But it *is* the first time I've been turned down by a woman I wanted to go out with as badly as I do with you.'

'And you expect me to believe that after tonight?'

'I guess not, but it's the truth.'

Lorinda turned away and wandered over to the window where she placed both hands on the sill and gazed down at the street below. She stiffened when he moved up behind her and tensed as he rested his hands on her shoulders, making her achingly aware of his nearness and the soft wind of his breath in her ear. Every instinct warned her to turn and run, but something stronger kept her in the circle of his arms as he turned her slowly to face him. The towelling gown fell open, exposing the creamy mounds of her breasts, but as she reached to pull the edges together, he restrained her with one hand while the other caressed her silken flesh.

By some trick, his hands once again looked lean and strong despite the brown age marks which she now knew were the result of skilfully applied make-up. She held her breath as one of those hands moved up to trace the edge of her hairline and gently push the thick curtain of hair back from her neck so he could touch his lips to the pulse fluttering wildly at her throat.

'You're so very lovely. I've wanted you in my arms like this from the moment I set eyes on you,' he breathed, and traced a line of kisses along her jawline. Another moment and his mouth would be on hers.

As his kisses seared her skin, her errant body demanded surrender, and instinctively she closed the small distance between them, feeling his taut muscles press against her thighs in response. For the first time she understood the meaning of the expression 'drugged by passion', for her will to resist was rapidly becoming submerged as wave after wave of desire raged through her.

Desperately she reminded herself of her vow to avoid emotional involvements. But what about physical involvement? She hadn't allowed for that. And yet in the split second left to her to decide on flight or surrender, she knew she couldn't have one without the other.

Panic-stricken, she ducked out from the circle of his arms and half ran across the room to cower behind the couch. Little caring whether she looked ridiculous or not, she picked up a table lamp and brandished it at him. 'Don't come near me!' she threatened.

Race spread his hands wide in a placatory gesture. 'Easy girl, no need to get violent! I thought you were as willing as I was—come to think of it, you damned well were. But if you want to back out now, I won't force you.'

'You won't touch me?'

He made the time-honoured gesture. 'Cross my heart. See, I'm sitting down nice and slow in this chair. Okay?'

Only when he was seated across the room did she feel safe enough to replace the lamp, but she stayed where she was behind the couch, feeling her heart hammering in her chest. 'What do you want from me?' she asked miserably.

'What any red-blooded man wants from a girl as desirable as you,' he said matter-of-factly. 'I wasn't allowing for your problem.'

She was baffled. 'What are you talking about? I don't have any problems.'

'Oh yes, you do, just now proved it. You aren't frigid, I'd stake my career on that after the last few minutes. So why is there such a blank where your love life ought to be?'

A chill racked her and her palms were damp, as if she had been found out in some way. 'I don't have to answer that,' she said defensively.

'No, you don't, because I think I know the answer. I've done some checking, you see, and I know that all your escorts are safe, undemanding and middle-aged. You didn't mind going about with me when you thought I was David Hewitt, down-at-heel actor. What I can't figure out is whether you're afraid of sex itself, or of ending up high and dry like your mother.'

Fury blazed in the tearful gaze she turned on him. 'You have no right to say things like that! Get out and leave me alone. I never want to see you again as long as I live!'

He rose easily. 'The truth is often painful, isn't it? But you will have to see me again, I'm afraid.'

'If you mean at the agency, I shan't be working there any more. I intend to find another job.'

He turned as he reached the door. 'Don't blame Max for what happened,' he cautioned. 'He was only doing what I instructed him to.'

'He could have refused.'

'I doubt it. Have you looked at the agency's books lately?'

Confused by this unexpected turn in the conversation, she shook her head. 'What does that have to do with anything?'

'A hell of a lot. The last few shows he's handled have just managed to break even. He needs my tour to balance the books again.'

'And you've been holding that over his head? That's the most despicable thing I've ever heard!'

'Maybe. But I've developed this bad habit of getting my own way. Nobody's been hurt.'

She could hardly believe her ears. 'Nobody's been hurt? What about me?'

His expression was derisive. 'So you've learned a few home truths about yourself. In the long run you may even thank me for it.'

Before she could find the words to respond to this unbelievable arrogance, he had gone, leaving her shaken and trembling. She sagged on to the couch and covered her face with her hands. He had no right to barge in here and say such things to her. They weren't even remotely true. Yet she couldn't deny that she was happiest in the company of men who posed no threat to her emotional stability—unlike Race Wolfendale, whose very existence seemed to threaten her.

Her skin burned in all the places he had touched her and she pulled her gown closer around herself. Why had he been so sure that she would see him again? It was possible, she supposed, for she knew she couldn't turn her back on Max if his business was indeed in trouble. She should have known there would be an explanation for what he did to her. But could she really forgive him for using her to save his business? Deep down she knew Max would only have agreed if he thought it was for her own good. He couldn't have foreseen how shattered she would be when she discovered the deception. David Hewitt had seemed so sweet and nice and ... yes, safe. There it was again! Damn Race Wolfendale for being right. She *did* stick to safe, undemanding men, but it wasn't because she was afraid of sex. But for her, it would be a total commitment and her fear of rejection afterwards ruled out any such relationships. Race didn't know about the suffering her mother endured after Rick left them, although it was no worse than all the nights Arna sat up waiting for a husband who had better places, and beds, to go to. Yes, Race was right when he said she was scared, but if he knew the whole story, he would see she had good reason to feel this way.

She sighed heavily. It looked as if the gypsy was right again. This tall dark stranger was going to be nothing but trouble. Nevertheless, she knew she would still go to the office tomorrow. Whatever his flaws, Max had always tried to do what was best for her, so she would give him the benefit of the doubt. But she would have as little as humanly possible to do with Race Wolfendale.

As she crawled into bed and waited a long time to fall into a troubled sleep, she couldn't know just how impossible this would turn out to be.

CHAPTER THREE

'RACE WOLFENDALE wants me to do *what*?'

Max patted her arm reassuringly. 'Please, Lori, it's not the end of the world. All he wants you to do is accompany him to Windi Bay to supervise the opening.'

'But I thought you were going to do that.'

Max looked embarrassed and shuffled the papers on his desk, a sure sign that he was uncomfortable about something. 'I was,' he conceded. 'But Race insists that you go instead. In fact . . .' He tailed off as if unsure how to tell her the rest.

'In fact what?' she prompted uneasily.

'He's . . . er . . . made it a condition of allowing this agency to handle the tour.'

Lorinda could hardly believe what he was saying. Knowing that the agency was in financial trouble and depending on his tour to get them back on their feet, Race had resorted to blackmail to get Max to agree to his terms. Tears of fury sprang to her eyes and she dashed them away with an impatient swipe of her hand.

Max misinterpreted the gesture and was immediately contrite. 'Don't cry, Lori. I didn't realise it would upset you like this.'

At once she lifted her head and faced him squarely. 'I'm not crying, darn it! But why is Race so determined to have me go with him? I thought I made it clear what I thought of him after his little masquerade—down-at-heel actor indeed!'

Max had the grace to look ashamed. 'I know, and I'm sorry I agreed to have any part of such a shabby

41

business. But he seemed so genuinely attracted to you and I could see you weren't going to give him a chance to get to know you any other way.'

She hated to disillusion Max, who looked for the best in everyone, but she was sure it was only Race's colossal ego which made him persist in chasing her after she'd made it clear that she wanted nothing to do with him. Suddenly, a ray of hope dawned on her. 'Wait a minute. Didn't Race sign the contract with us before he came to Australia?'

Max frowned. 'Yes, of course, but I'm afraid the terms of the agreement allow him to choose his own staff, and he's chosen you. Unless I agree, we're breaching the contract and he says in that case he'd have no hesitation in backing out.'

From what she'd seen of Race Wolfendale so far she was positive he meant what he said. But how could he be so cruel? He knew she didn't want to go out with him, although he didn't know the real reason. He thought she was man-shy, and it was better he should believe that than think her all kinds of a fool because she was being influenced by such a crazy thing as a gypsy's prediction. If only this tour wasn't so important to the agency! Then she remembered she had only Race's word for that. Perhaps it wasn't as bad as he had suggested.

'Max,' she ventured hopefully, 'how much is the agency depending on this tour?'

Her boss looked at her sharply, then his features crumpled into a look of such despondency that she knew what his answer was going to be, even before he said, 'This tour is everything to us financially. I don't think there would be a Metropolitan Casting for much longer without it. I didn't want to tell you, but I should have known you'd guess the truth.'

It was her turn to offer a reassuring hand. 'It's all

right, Max. I just wish you'd told me, that's all. We would have worked something out—I could have taken a pay cut, or something.'

He smiled wryly. 'I couldn't very well ask you to do that. You get little enough as it is.'

'But I'm getting valuable training here,' she reminded him. 'I haven't forgotten that you gave me a job when I had nothing to offer a prospective employer but some average grades at school. And you've done a lot for Mum and me since . . . my father left. Now it looks like I have a chance to repay you.' Unconsciously she squared her shoulders. 'If Mr Wolfendale wants me as his assistant, I hereby volunteer for the job.'

His relief was written on his face, but he quickly masked it with an expression of concern. 'You're sure you want to go through with this?'

She nodded. 'I'm sure. What I'm not sure about is what possible use I can be at the resort. From what I know about the place, I'd say they already have more staff than guests.'

'That's the kind of image they want to create,' he agreed. 'They're catering to the rich and famous, so it's important that they want for nothing. So you can treat it as a working holiday—let's hope, with more holiday than work.'

'I could use a rest,' she said wistfully. 'But I wish Windi Bay wasn't so far away.'

'You're worried about your mother?' She nodded. 'Well, how would it be if I promise to visit her as often as I can get away?'

'Oh, Max, that would be great! She's very happy now she's settled at the convalescent home in the mountains, but if you could spare the time to visit her . . .'

'I'll make the time,' he said firmly. 'The main thing

is, you're to go away, enjoy yourself and come back here as brown as a berry. You can call Arna whenever you like—and put it on Wolfendale's account,' he said recklessly.

She laughed. 'I'll do that!' It would be little enough repayment for the way he had treated her. In the meantime, all she had to do was keep her personal feelings in check while she carried out the duties of his assistant. Not that it would be easy, she reflected, since he had already given her so much cause to dislike him. First he had deceived her by posing as a harmless old actor in order to worm his way into her confidence. Now he was using Max's misfortune to trap her into going to the Barrier Reef resort with him.

It was true, he had said he liked her and wanted to get to know her better. At least he claimed that was his motive, but surely any decent man would have taken no for an answer by now. Obviously, Race Wolfendale didn't fit that description. There was another description he *did* fit, though, and she shuddered every time she recalled the gypsy's warning that she would meet a tall dark stranger who would take from her something she valued. Race was not only tall and dark and a stranger but had already taken away her peace of mind with his persistent intrusions into her life. What more could he take from her?

She was about to go back to her desk when Max caught her arm. 'Lori, I'm a pretty poor substitute for a father, but I've always tried to give you the best guidance I could. Now here's another piece of advice for what it's worth. I know Wolfendale's reputation and I want your promise that you'll come straight back here the moment he starts getting out of line. Contract or no, your happiness is more important to me than any business.'

It was a long speech for her usually taciturn boss

and she found herself blinking away tears. She knew how important the agency was to Max. It would break his heart to have to start all over again, but it touched her deeply to know that he would do it rather than allow her to get hurt. 'I promise,' she said huskily, and hurried out of his office.

The next twenty-four hours went past in a blur. There was so much to do, not only preparing for the trip but making sure that her work was up to date before she left. She arranged to have the mail held at the post office and stopped various deliveries. Luckily, she didn't have to worry about the flat or her car while she and her mother were away; dear kind Mrs Clarke was only to happy to keep her eye on things. 'Else what are neighbours for?' she told Lorinda.

That left only her personal packing to be done. What on earth did one take to an exclusive island resort? she pondered as she surveyed the contents of her wardrobe. There had never been much money left for fancy clothes, even after she started working, but she was handy with a needle and enjoyed sewing, so she was able to dress well even on her tight budget.

Thoughtfully, she tapped a fingernail against her teeth. Since there was very little real work involved on the trip, she would manage with a couple of uncrushable day dresses. Then she would need a swimsuit and some sort of cover-up against the fiery Queensland sun, and a sunhat, of course. Evenings would be the real problem. She would be expected to dress up, yet nothing she owned could measure up to the designer gowns the wealthy paying guests would be wearing. She sighed and wondered again why Race had to be so stubborn about dragging her along.

Suddenly she had a deliciously wicked idea. Since she didn't want to go with him, why not pay him back by being as dowdy as possible? What a joke that would be! Did she have the nerve to go through with it? Thinking of how he had treated her strengthened her resolve. Of course she did—the question was, how? Race was coming to pick her up this afternoon to drive them to the airport, so that didn't leave her much time for scheming.

Then she had another inspiration—she could take her mother's clothes instead of her own. They were far from dowdy, but were much more conservative than the styles she normally wore, and of course, they were far too old for her. She knew Arna wouldn't mind her borrowing a few things since she wouldn't be needing many clothes while she was convalescing. It was perfect!

Trembling with excitement at the prospect of getting her revenge on Race, she hurried into her mother's bedroom and flung open the wardrobe door. Swiftly she chose a grey pin-striped cotton suit which would be light enough for day wear, her mother's demure navy satin swimdress, a long black evening skirt and high-necked white blouse. Fortunately, she and her mother were almost the same size, although Lorinda was the taller. The only things she would need of her own were her shoes.

She had just spread the borrowed clothes out on her bed alongside her open suitcase when the doorbell rang. Something in the arrogantly persistent pealing of the bell told her it was Race Wolfendale, even though it was much too early, she wasn't expecting him until after lunch. The bell went on ringing, and remembering the previous evening, she knew it was not going to stop until she answered the door.

Seething, she stalked to the door and flung it wide. 'I thought it would be you!'

'That's a nice welcome from my assistant,' he drawled in his broad Californian accent, and strode into the flat without waiting for an invitation.

'The choice was yours, not mine. You made sure I had no option but to agree, after all.'

'Sure looks that way,' he agreed with maddening good humour. His gaze travelled past her to the clothes spread out on the bed, plainly visible through the open bedroom door. 'I hoped you'd be ready by now so we could get an early start.'

'Well, as you can see, I'm still packing,' she retorted.

He shrugged. 'Don't mind me, carry on.'

Lorinda was about to snap back that she would get the job done much faster without his disturbing presence, then thought better of it and turned back to the bedroom. Perhaps ignoring him would make the point for her.

She should have known it wouldn't be that simple. As soon as she bent over the suitcase her sixth sense told her he was right behind her, and every nerve ending quivered with the awareness that he was near. None of the famous people she had worked with up to now had exuded such a tangible *presence*. The very force of his personality charged the air like the atmosphere before an electrical storm, and she felt it particularly strongly now as he came up behind her. His steely gaze surveyed her mother's clothes laid out on the bed and she began to wish she hadn't conceived such a childish idea. It was an effort to stop her hand from shaking as she reached for the black evening skirt.

'Leave it!' he commanded, and she dropped the garment as if it was red-hot.

She whirled on him. 'Just because you managed to blackmail me into going with you that doesn't give you any right to order me around!'

Defiantly she reached for the skirt again, and winced as his hand clamped over her wrist like a shackle. 'Where I come from, blackmail's an ugly word,' Race said dangerously. 'I simply exercised my contractual right to choose my own assistant. And the one I chose does not go around dressing like her grandmother.'

His comment came so near to the truth that she flushed scarlet. 'You're talking nonsense,' she said, wishing that for once she was a more convincing liar.

'Am I? Then let's see what else you've got in here.' He dropped her arm and strode over to the wardrobe, where he began pulling out garments and tossing them on to the bed. 'You can take this one, and this one. Ah, this is more like it.' He threw a silky evening dress in vivid turquoise across to her and she caught it in nerveless fingers. 'That should do very nicely for opening night.'

Fuming, she restrained an urge to fling herself at him and beat that barrel chest with her fists. She would do about as much damage as a fly, she knew, and only give him further cause to mock her. 'Is there anything else?' she asked coldly.

He seemed impervious to her anger. 'Just one thing.' To her horror, he began opening drawers and riffling through them. The sight of her piles of delicate frilled underwear seemed to affect him not at all, and she wondered spitefully how many women he had undressed to achieve such casual familiarity with their intimate apparel. Deftly he continued choosing garments until he had selected her entire travel wardrobe. He paused when he came to her one-piece swimsuit, which he studied critically, then tossed aside in favour of her white crocheted bikini. 'There, that ought to do it. Pack those and we'll be on our way.'

Without a backward glance he strode out of the room and Lorinda heard him moving around the kitchen, where the clink of cups and kettle told her he was making coffee. She sank onto a chair and stared at the pile of clothes on the bed. She ought to do something about folding and packing them, but she needed a moment to regroup her defences. She felt somehow violated, as if by going through her intimate possessions, Race had plundered her very soul. She was sorely tempted to tell him she wasn't going anywhere with him and he could do what he pleased about it, but then she thought about Max. If Race refused to appear at Windi Bay, Max would have to pay the resort a lot of money in compensation, and that would be the last straw for his business. He had been willing to sacrifice the agency rather than see her get hurt, but she knew she couldn't let him do it. Whatever it cost her, she would have to see this thing through.

Like a robot, she folded the clothes Race had chosen and packed them into the suitcase. Luckily she was already dressed for the trip in a lemon and grey two-piece suit of uncrushable fabric, a decision she was now thankful for, so there was nothing left to do but carry the suitcase into the living room.

Race was sprawled in an armchair, sipping coffee, and he rose as she came in. 'All ready?' She nodded tautly, and he handed her a steaming mug. 'I thought you'd appreciate this before we go.'

The liquid scalded her throat, but she swallowed it valiantly. At least it absolved her from the need to make conversation with him. In her present mood, she knew that if she said anything at all she wouldn't stop until she had told him a few home truths, which wouldn't help the situation at all.

After a few moments of emotion-charged silence, Race set his cup down carefully. 'Look, Lorinda, we're going to be together for the next week or so.

Don't you think it would be more pleasant if we behaved like adults to one another?'

'You should have thought about that before you made me come on this trip against my will!'

He grinned unexpectedly and she felt something very strange happen inside her. 'Is it really such an unpleasant prospect—spending some time at an exclusive island resort?'

'No,' she admitted reluctantly. 'It's just . . . well, I'd like to know why you were so insistent that I was the one to go with you.'

'I've already told you. I want to get to know you and you won't even give me a chance when I ask nicely. Besides . . .' he hesitated uncharacteristically.

In spite of herself, she was curious to know the rest. 'Besides what?'

'I want to help you, dammit. You're much too beautiful to waste your life because you have a hang-up about men.'

Lorinda almost spilled her coffee. 'I do not have a hang-up about men!' she protested hotly.

'Methinks the lady doth protest too much,' he quoted softly, and she was immediately reminded of him in the role of 'David Hewitt'. He gestured around the living room. 'I notice you have plenty of pictures of your mother, but none of your father. Why?'

'I don't think that's any of your business.'

'You're forgetting I already know what a rough deal your father gave you and your mother,' he reminded her. 'Is that it, Lorinda? When you go out with those nice, safe middle-aged men, are you looking for a father figure?'

Angrily she jumped to her feet. 'You may enjoy playing amateur psychiatrist,' she seethed, 'but I don't enjoy being your patient. You know very little about me, so I'll thank you to keep opinions like that one to yourself!'

'I see,' he murmured, and she was afraid her outburst had only convinced him he had guessed correctly. He was not to know that she chose her escorts, not for their fatherly qualities, for that had never entered her head. Rather, it was because there was no chance at all of her becoming emotionally involved with them, which she had vowed never to do with anyone.

Maybe it was a good thing if Race attributed her dislike of him to a so-called father fixation. At least he would never know that she resisted him so strongly because of that stupid gypsy prediction. If he found out about that he would mock her unmercifully and no doubt pursue her all the harder. Then what would happen to the wall she had so carefully built around her emotions? For she already knew what Race did not—that, far from finding him repulsive, she found him much too attractive by halves. And she had a lifetime of experience to warn her that whenever she allowed herself to get too close to someone, they would leave or she would. In her experience, friendships, and even love, were temporary and only led to heartbreak when they inevitably ended.

Race said nothing more until she had rinsed the coffee cups and locked up the flat after a last look around to make sure she hadn't forgotten anything or left anything switched on. At last there was nothing to do except follow him down to the street where, he informed her, he had parked the Porsche he'd been renting during his stay in Sydney.

'I'm sorry if I touched a nerve earlier,' he said as he stowed her luggage alongside his in the car.

'You didn't touch any nerve, as you call it, because there's nothing to touch! I've heard that life in

Hollywood revolves around psychiatric analysis, but I can assure you, it's different here, so you may as well stop digging.'

'As it happens, I've never seen an analyst in my life,' he said imperturbably. 'But just because you don't believe in it, it doesn't mean you don't have your share of problems here, too.'

If he used that word once more, she would scream! she thought. If only she'd been an old maid with grey hair and hornrimmed glasses, maybe he wouldn't be so keen to find out what was going on inside her head. She thought fleetingly of all the women in Australia who would give their eye teeth to be in her shoes right now, heading off to a tropical paradise with the world's most eligible man. She should be flattered and thrilled that he had singled her out for attention. Instead, she wished fervently that he had chosen someone else—anyone else. In desperation, she turned in the car seat to face him. 'For the last time,' she said with deadly calm, 'I don't have any "problems," as you put it, and I'm not anti-men.' Just anti-Race Wolfendale, she thought silently. 'So please can we drop the subject so I can get on with being your assistant. That *was* what you wanted me along for, wasn't it?'

His expression lightened and he flashed that famous lopsided smile which did such peculiar things to her insides. 'O.K., if that's the way you want it, honey. I just have this fascination with what makes people tick. I guess it's the actor in me—always trying to understand a character from the inside. It's become kind of a habit. And you are the most intriguing person I've met in a long while with your . . . sorry, I'm doing it again, aren't I?'

'Yes, you are,' she concurred.

'Well, I do want to be friends with you. In fact, I'd

like to be a lot more than friends, so I'll do my level best not to analyse you any more. Fair enough?'

She could hardly disagree without sounding churlish. Still, she was baffled as to how he had managed to turn the situation around so completely that she not only heard herself forgiving him for his arrogant behaviour but agreeing to give him the chance to get to know her better—which was what he had wanted all along. Did he always get his own way? she wondered, bemused. There was no doubt he could be devastatingly charming, as she was finding out now, but then he *was* an accomplished actor. The charm was probably part of his act.

Although she had pretended ignorance to Marla, she *had* seen two of his films. In *The Iron Cross* he had portrayed an unrepentant war criminal and had succeeded in making the audience hate him. In the other film, *Beloved Stranger*, he played a completely opposite role as a handsome marathon runner torn between love and his athletic career. He had won an Oscar for that role, she recalled. So how could she be sure that the charm he was now displaying to her was any more real than what she had seen on film? She would have to take everything he said with a very large grain of salt.

Suddenly she became aware of the route they were taking. 'This isn't the way to the airport,' she said in surprise. 'We should have turned left at the last intersection.'

'I know,' he grinned. 'But I thought you'd like to say goodbye to your mother before we left. That was the real reason why I came by early.'

'But have you any idea of how far it is to the Blue Mountains from here? We'll never be back in time for our flight!'

'Relax. I switched our reservations to a later flight,

so we'll have all the time we need. I thought you'd be pleased about the detour.'

Of course she was pleased. She had telephoned her mother this morning to say goodbye, but it wasn't the same as saying it in person, and both of them had been reluctant to hang up. Even though she wasn't going away for very long, it was the first time they had been apart for more than a night or two since Rick left, and both felt the parting acutely.

Still, she couldn't help being concerned about Arna seeing her with Race like this. Despite her own experience of marriage, Arna Fleming was an incurable romantic and was bound to misinterpret a joint visit. There didn't seem to be much she could do about it now, so, to distract herself, she asked. 'Don't you find it odd driving on the "wrong" side of the road?'

Given the masterful way he was handling the powerful car in the heavy traffic, it was a foolish question, but to her relief, he decided to humour her. 'Luckily I've done enough travelling around the world to be comfortable on either side of the road. Added to which, after the freeways in L.A., your highways are a breeze.'

'Is that where you live?'

'Mostly. I have two homes—an apartment in North Hollywood which I use when I'm working, and a house on the coast in Santa Barbara which I get away to as often as I can.'

'The Santa Barbara house sounds nice,' she said a little wistfully.

'I think so. It's a big old Spanish villa called Casa Juniperos. Behind, it has the Santa Ynez Mountains and in front, there's the Pacific.'

'I'm surprised you can bear to leave it,' Lorinda murmured dreamily.

He appraised her in surprise. 'So you're *not* as tough as you pretend! I'll bet you love the sea as much as I do.'

'I thought you weren't going to psycho-analyse me,' she challenged.

His glance flicked from the road to her face and back to the road. 'We weren't. But you started it by asking about me, so fair's fair. Besides, the sea is safe enough territory, isn't it?'

'Not in Australia,' she chuckled, 'We have these large, toothy fish called sharks.'

'That wasn't what I meant and you know it. Lorinda, why are you so reluctant to open up about your own feelings, even when it's something as harmless as whether you like the sea or not?'

They were back on that tack again, she thought in dismay, and she could see she'd better defuse the situation in a hurry or they would be arguing again. 'All right, so I would dearly like to live near the sea,' she confessed with a sharp edge of irritation in her voice. 'I just never had the chance, that's all.'

'Then you must come to the States and stay awhile at the villa,' he said firmly. Since there was very little chance she would ever be able to afford such a trip, she saw no harm in agreeing with him, and saw him tilt an eyebrow in surprise when she murmured that she would like that.

After that she became so engrossed in her own thoughts that she hardly noticed the miles slipping by and looked up to find they were already climbing the foothills of the Blue Mountains.

'How did you know where my mother was staying?' she asked.

'Max told me. When he mentioned she'd been ill, I said I'd like you to see her before you left. He promised to let the Windi Bay management know that we'd be arriving later than scheduled.'

She frowned. 'I thought I was the one supposed to be doing the errands?'

In answer Race slammed on the brakes so hard that she was jolted forward and, but for the seatbelt, would have catapulted through the front windscreen. Luckily, there was no one behind them to object as Race steered the car on to the edge of the road. Then he turned and took her by both shoulders, shaking her impatiently. 'You are the most infuriating female!' he rasped. 'Every time I try to do something nice for you, I get kicked in the teeth!'

The idea of someone as petite as herself inflicting physical injury on someone of Race's superb condition and build was so amusing she began to laugh.

'What's so damned funny?' he demanded.

'The idea of m-me k-kicking you in the t-teeth,' she gasped through her laughter.

A spark of amusement flared in the dark gaze. 'Oh, so you thinks it's funny, do you? Well, see what you think of this!'

Before she realised what he meant to do, he had drawn her against him and brought his mouth down hard over hers. The diagonal strap of her seatbelt bit into the tender flesh of her breasts, but she was oblivious to anything but the tide of emotion sweeping over her. The last time Race had tried to kiss her, she had successfully avoided him, but this time he gave her no chance to escape. By denying him her lips on that occasion, she had been left with a gnawing hunger to know his kiss, deny it as she might—and now that hunger was being fed with a vengeance! She had seen him kiss his leading ladies on screen and had shivered with vicarious delight, along with thousands of other women, but nothing could have prepared her for the reality. A heady tingling sensation began at the back of her neck where his fingers were twined in her hair, and continued through her body like a current of electricity as his mouth plundered hers.

All common sense told her she should end this, but her body had ideas of its own. To her chagrin, she found herself responding with an abandoned eagerness which she seemed powerless to restrain. Race's weight held one arm pinned against the soft leather of the seat, but her other hand was free and, almost of its own accord, it came up to wind around Race's shoulders and pull his body even closer against her.

The blast of a car horn shattered the magic moment and Race pulled away from her slowly, like a magnet pulling away from metal. A huge semi-trailer was almost on top of their car, its driver impatiently leaning on his horn to remind them that he was unable to pass on the narrow stretch of road, because of the volume of traffic coming the other way.

Without a word, Race slammed the Porsche into gear and pulled out on to the road in front of the truck, taking advantage of the fast pick-up of the superbly tuned engine to get well ahead of the hauler.

While he completed this manoeuvre, Lorinda was grateful for the few minutes' respite to gather her whirling thoughts. What on earth had happened to her in those few minutes? Her heart was fluttering in her chest like a bird against a window and her breath came in ragged gasps. It was the first time anyone had kissed her like that, and the worst of it was, she liked it.

Race knew it, too, because he finally slowed the car and glanced at her. 'I was wasting my time analysing you,' he admitted. 'I should just have kissed you—it gave me all the answers I needed.'

'Such as?' she asked warily.

'Well, the iceberg has a heart, for one thing. And you're not so impervious to me as you want me to believe.'

What could she say? She could hardly deny that he had affected her beyond belief with his kiss. 'You— you caught me off guard,' she said weakly. 'It was very unfair.'

'There's an answer to that—something about love and war,' he pointed out. 'At first I thought it was going to be war between us. Now I'm not so sure.'

Neither was she, she realised. But there was no way she was going to let him know that. So she kept silent as he swung the car into the driveway of Wentworth House, the convalescent home where her mother was staying.

It was as bad as Lorinda had feared. As soon as Arna saw them together, she brightened considerably and referred often to 'you two' in her conversation.

Lorinda was conscious of the stir Race caused by his arrival, but he seemed merely amused by the frequent excuses the nurses found to cross the lawn to where they were sitting beside the pool. Lorinda felt horribly uncomfortable, but Race himself, and Arna—once married to an entertainer—took the attention in their stride and carried on chatting like old friends. At last Race stood up and reached for Lorinda's hand. 'Time we were getting to the airport, honey.'

She couldn't very well ignore his hand without causing a scene, and it was difficult to scramble up from the low chaise-longue without assistance, so she took his hand just long enough to rise with dignity, then tugged free.

When she bent to kiss her mother, Race moved discreetly away a few paces. 'Have a wonderful time, darling,' Arna instructed as their cheeks touched.

'Don't worry about me. Just concentrate on getting well.'

'Oh, I'm not worried, darling. Not now I've seen how nice your Race Wolfendale is.'

Lorinda sighed. 'He's not *my* Race Wolfendale, Mum. I'm just his assistant while he's here, that's all.'

'Of course, I understand. "Just good friends", we used to say.'

What was the use? Arna was determined to pair them off and Lorinda could hardly argue with her in her present state of health. 'All right, Mum. We're just good friends, then. But don't go getting your hopes up—I'm not about to head for the altar yet.'

'Good. Give me time to get out of here first, so I can be a mother-of-the-bride you can be proud of.'

'Mother!'

She was about to turn away in exasperation when her mother winked conspiratorially. 'I think he's wonderful, darling. So tall and dark and all!'

The hairs on the back of Lorinda's neck prickled with nerves as she walked back to the car with Race. It was bad enough to have Arna matchmaking between them so eagerly, but why did she have to make the comment about Race being tall and dark?

It was as if she had been given a timely reminder of the gypsy's warning. She was overwhelmed by a sudden, irrational urge to turn and run, and if it hadn't been for the consequences to Max's business, she felt sure she would have done so. But he was depending on her and she couldn't let him down after all he had done for her. Still, she wondered how in the world she was going to survive the next few days.

CHAPTER FOUR

As it turned out, it looked as though she would have nothing to worry about. By the time their jet touched down at Cairns airport and they switched to the helicopter which would fly them out to Windi Bay, Race had undergone a startling transformation.

From teasing playboy, he had changed into a serious professional, discussing aspects of his show with her in a detached manner which made her wonder if she had dreamed the scene at her flat when he had riffled through her personal possessions, or the heady moment when he had kissed her on the way to the Blue Mountains.

She risked a sideways glance at his dark head bent over an orchestral score, and the tingling sensation which immediately vibrated through her body told her that she hadn't imagined any of it. His fiery kiss was printed on her lips like a brand and she touched curious fingers to her mouth, almost surprised to find no tangible mark.

Quickly she turned her attention to the Barrier Reef, which lay like a jewelled necklace on an azure velvet cloth beneath them, and strained to pick out the new resort from the myriad islands clustered below. She had read a lot about Windi Bay in order to prepare the press releases before Race arrived, but no amount of words could have prepared her for the spellbinding beauty of the resort, which became apparent as they approached it.

Windi Bay was the only habitation on a tiny coral cay some sixteen miles north-east of Cairns, she recalled. From the air as they came nearer, she could see the centre thickly timbered with lush tropical vegetation, fringed by a garland of silver sand. As they hovered over the helipad, she could see thick stands of spiky pandanus palms swaying in the helicopter's downdraft.

Then there was a jolt and they had landed. Eagerly she accepted the pilot's hand to jump down and crouched until she was clear of the whirling rotors, then she straightened up to drink in the panoply of sights, sounds and scents of her first tropical island. The oven-like blast of heat which welled up towards them made the trees shimmer and dance before her eyes and she shaded her brow with one hand.

The helicopter pilot, Chuck Rider came up behind her. 'Hot enough for you?'

'It's wonderful,' she enthused, 'just the way I imagined a tropical island to be. The only thing is . . .'

'Yes, ma'am?'

'Where *is* the resort? I couldn't pick it out from the air.'

The pilot grinned. 'That's the general idea. It's there all right, but designed and built to blend in with the character of the island. As soon as I've unloaded your luggage, I'll show you the way.'

Before he could return with their cases, a man emerged from the sheltering palms and hurried towards them. He was in his fifties but tanned and fit-looking, Lorinda noted. From the badge he wore on the lapel of his impeccably tailored safari suit, she saw he was the resort manager. He extended a hand to Race and said in German-accented tones, 'Welcome to Windi Bay, Mr Wolfendale. I'm Gerhardt Muller, the manager here.'

'Pleased to meet you,' Race responded. 'This is Lorinda Fleming from Metropolitan Casting. You two have met by phone, I gather.'

Lorinda smiled and nodded at the manager and was embarrassed to see his eyes appraise her with frank appreciation. But his words of welcome were innocent enough and he devoted all his attention to Race as they walked towards the hotel, leaving Lorinda to follow in their wake.

Here on the ground, she could see why the resort was almost invisible from the air. The grounds were criss-crossed with covered walkways, and, like the buildings, the roofs were thatched to blend in with the surroundings. She caught her breath as they entered the main building and Gerhardt Muller looked back at her in understanding. 'It is very impressive,' he said in answer to her unspoken thoughts. 'Especially the first time you see it.'

From the outside, the building's timber and thatch design made it look almost primitive, but inside it lived up to its promise as the most luxurious resort in the region. They entered a lobby whose ceiling soared cathedral-like overhead and passed between glass cases of intriguing Melanesian handicrafts which Lorinda resolved to study more closely as soon as she had a chance.

Beyond the lobby was a spacious guest lounge, its sides open to the cooling sea breezes. All the furniture was made of woven cane painted a sparkling white and the walls were hung with more native handicrafts.

Although the resort was not officially open for another few days, a number of guests were already in residence, and there was a slight stir amongst them as they recognised Race. She should be getting used to the attention he attracted wherever he went, she knew, but she doubted whether she would ever accept it with the same effortless grace that he did.

'After you have registered,' Gerhardt Muller told them, 'I will escort you to your suites. I am sure it has been a long day for you, madam, with all the travelling.'

The manager's courtly manner and delightful accent charmed Lorinda, but judging from Race's frown, he was not so impressed. Well, bully for him! Maybe it was time he realised she was a passably attractive woman with a life of her own, and not just the neurotic female he seemed to think her. She gave the manager a grateful smile. 'You're very kind, Mr Muller—or should I call you Herr Muller?'

In response, the man raised her hand as if to kiss it and half-bowed, but released her before the gesture was complete. 'Why trouble with either, Miss Fleming? I would be honoured if you would call me Gerhardt.'

As she laughingly agreed and, in turn, urged him to call her Lorinda, she had the satisfaction of seeing Race's frown grow even deeper.

Reception formalities over, they were shown to their suites, two of a small group in a long, low line joined to the main building by a thatch-roofed walkway. Gerhardt assured them there was additional accommodation besides these private suites, but even when fully booked, Windi Bay was only designed to cater for a limited number of people. At fabulous cost, Lorinda remembered from earlier briefings on the resort.

With a flourish, Gerhardt flung open one of the doors, then left her to explore the suite, whose very simplicity belied the expense which had gone into decorating it. There was an entrance foyer leading to the bedsitting area, which was large and furnished in island style. Cool ceramic tiles underfoot made everything shimmer with colour and added to the feeling of spaciousness.

Another door opened on to a roomy bathroom and she ran an appreciative hand over the mother-of-pearl adorning the walls. Even the soap-holders were made out of seashells, polished until they glistened. But the greatest delight was the balcony opening off the main room. It was also tiled and furnished with rattan chairs and a table and shaded by overhanging palms planted just beyond it.

Beyond that was the beach, garlanded by the sparkling perfection of the coral-studded sea. It was late in the day and the huge orange orb of the sun balanced on the horizon, flooding the ocean with gold. As Lorinda leaned far out over the low wall separating the balcony from the beach, she heard the murmur of voices from the suite next door and looked up to see Race standing on his own balcony, not a dozen feet away. But he was not admiring the view, she realised with a start as her wandering gaze encountered his. She pulled quickly back and returned to her bedroom to unpack.

It was dark by the time she had finished and she was just about to step outside in search of the dining room when she heard Race's voice. 'I'm sure Miss Fleming is too tired to come down to dinner this evening, so would you have something sent up for her?'

'My pleasure, Mr Wolfendale,' came Gerhardt Muller's voice, and she heard the manager's footsteps disappearing in the direction of the main building.

'Oh, I didn't see you there,' said Race as he turned to find her standing in the open doorway.

'I gathered that, or you might have troubled to ask me whether I was tired or not before making up my mind for me.'

'Well, aren't you?' he asked equably, and rested one hand on the doorframe so she was trapped in the circle of his arm.

Once again she was achingly conscious of his nearness and she had to make an effort to keep her breathing even. As it was, her voice sounded unnaturally husky to her own ears. 'As it happens, yes, too tired to argue with you, luckily. But I do wish you'd stop trying to tell me how I feel.'

He leaned closer until her nostrils were assailed with the sharp citrus tang of his aftershave lotion, and she had the heady feeling that he was going to kiss her again. But he only said, 'I'll stop when you admit that I'm right and you're wrong.'

The hypnotic sensation evaporated at once and she ran a distracted hand through her hair. 'So we're back to that again! I thought when you were being so businesslike on the plane that we might be getting somewhere.'

'Not where I had in mind,' Race grinned, then his expression became serious. 'But that was before you went all weak at the knees over Mr Muller—"or should I say Herr Muller?" ' he mimicked.

'Oh, stop it! Just because I'm not attracted to you you've convinced yourself that there's something wrong with *me*. You're the actor who loves quotations. Try the one about the fault not being in our stars but in ourselves.'

'Or the one I gave you before, about protesting too much,' he shot back. 'I was right, though, you *are* tired. We'll talk in the morning.'

Then he was gone to his own suite, leaving Lorinda leaning weakly against the doorframe. Slowly she turned back inside, closed the door and walked out to the balcony, where she sank down on to one of the rattan chairs, not willing to admit even to herself that she felt cheated because he hadn't kissed her. Much more of this and he would have her believing there *was* something wrong with her! Damn him! Deep down, she knew she was attracted to him and he knew it too, for her response to his kiss had betrayed her. But despite that, there was no way she was going to let herself become involved with him.

He thought he had solved the puzzle of her resistance in her preference for safe, undemanding escorts. What would he say if he knew it was because a gypsy had warned her about him—and because she knew in her heart that loving an entertainer, even an internationally acclaimed one like Race, could only lead to the sort of heartache her mother had suffered? Was that what the gypsy had been trying to warn her against?

She shivered, and not only with the effect of the rapidly cooling night air. There was only one way to keep Race from guessing the truth, and that was to encourage his belief in her so-called father fixation. She certainly found Gerhardt Muller charming, but the idea that she was attracted to him had not even entered her head until Race planted the idea there. Perhaps if she acted as though Gerhardt attracted her, it would prevent Race from discovering the real reason she didn't want an involvement with him—that if she let herself, she could fall in love with him, and there was no surer route to a broken heart.

Her reverie was interrupted by a knock on the door and she caught her breath, feeling her heart begin to race. Then she sagged like a pricked balloon when a man's voice called, 'Room Service'. She opened the door and a waiter wheeled in a small trolley set for one.

When he had gone she lifted the silver covers to find avocado stuffed with seafood, a crisp green salad and a slice of creamy continental torte, along with a half bottle of French champagne. As she surveyed the feast she wished she had more appetite to do the food justice. But she was only able to nibble at the salad and didn't feel she could face the rich dessert at all.

However, she did drink a glass of the champagne, hoping it would help her to sleep after the tensions of the day.

When she had finished, she left the trolley outside her door and returned to run a hot bath into which she scattered a generous handful of fragrant bath crystals she found in a milk glass urn on the edge of the bath.

By the time she had soaked for half an hour in the scented tub, she felt almost too languid to move. But habit was too strong and she forced herself to give her long tresses their ritual brushing before she climbed into bed.

Her sleep was tormented by a dream in which she was chased by a gypsy woman screaming warnings at her. As she fled from the woman she ran headlong into the arms of a dark-haired man with burning coals for eyes. She awoke to find herself sitting bolt upright in bed with the morning sun casting golden streamers across the bedspread.

There was a gentle tap at the door and it opened to admit a young woman who introduced herself as the chambermaid, Susie. Judging by her honey-coloured skin and huge darkly luminous eyes, she came from one of the islands to the north of Australia. Susie served Lorinda a steaming cup of tea and shyly informed her that Mr Wolfendale had requested that she join him for breakfast on his balcony.

By the time Lorinda went next door to Race's suite she was suitably dressed in a printed polyester shirtwaister and neat white low-heeled sandals and her hair caught up in a knot at the nape of her neck. The cool upswept hairstyle and absence of stockings were the only concessions she had made to being on a tropical island.

When she reached his door, she found a note pinned to it. 'Gone jogging. Make yourself at home, R.W.'

Hesitantly, she pushed open the door, but he was still out, so she made her way through the suite to the balcony where she found the table had been set for two. A morning newspaper—flown in by helicopter from the mainland, she guessed—lay folded on the covered tray, so she opened it and tried to make sense of the headlines, but her attention kept wandering to the broad expanse of silvery beach beyond the balcony.

After a few minutes, the figure she had been unconsciously seeking came into sight. As he jogged effortlessly along the sand, his long legs, rippling with well developed muscles, ate up the beach and his broad, tanned torso glistened from his exertion. He wore nothing but a pair of black swim-shorts and he must have been in the water already, because they clung to him like a second skin. His hair was also slick with water. He waved as he caught sight of her on the balcony.

Unnerved by the surge of emotion she felt when he came into view, she was determined not to wave back and kept her eyes downcast on the front page of the newspaper, although the print swam senselessly before her eyes.

She was showered with droplets of water as he vaulted over the wall of the balcony and threw himself into the other chair. 'Let me guess. There's been another coup in South America, a riot in Europe and another skirmish in the Middle East.'

'You shouldn't be so flippant about it,' she admonished as she folded the paper and set it aside.

'I'm on a tropical island, the day is positively golden and I'm about to have breakfast with a beautiful girl. Is it any wonder I'm counting my blessings?'

She said nothing and busied herself with uncovering the breakfast tray and playing 'mother' with the coffee pot. The croissants were still warm and crumbling from the oven, and the tray held a selection of conserves, fresh fruit and Danish pastries. 'Not exactly diet food,' she said, thinking aloud.

'I doubt if you ever have to worry on that score,' he said, eyeing her bare brown legs crossed demurely at the knee.

Lorinda resisted an impulse to pull the skirt down over her knees and began to spread apricot conserve on to a croissant. 'Why did you want to see me?' she asked in an effort to steer the conversation on to a professional level.

To her surprise, he picked up her cue. 'I wanted to check on the details of this morning's press conference. How many journalists are we expecting?'

'I don't have the file—it's in my suite, but from memory there are a dozen papers, dailies and weeklies, and three national magazines represented.'

'Any wire services?'

'Both of them, and one commercial TV station from the mainland. They're a national network, so we should get round-Australia coverage.'

He nodded, digesting this. 'And what time is Simone arriving?'

She felt an inexplicable pang when he mentioned the exotic dancer who was to be Race's supporting act. 'Do you know Miss Dyson?' she asked.

'We've worked together in Hawaii and Vegas,' he confirmed. 'You could say we ... know ... one another pretty well.'

Why this discovery should disturb her, she couldn't imagine. She had never met the dancer, although she knew a lot about her professional background, having prepared biographies on both her and Race to hand out to the press. So she knew Simone Dyson was an olive-skinned, sloe-eyed beauty who held audiences spellbound with her dance routines performed with flaming torches and live snakes. It had never occurred to her that Simone and Race might be friends—or even lovers—and for some reason she found the idea oddly disquieting, although she had no justification for feeling that way.

At Race's request, they spent the next hour rehearsing the questions he was most likely to be asked during the press conference. They also discussed how much he could safely reveal about his next film, which was under wraps since contracts had not been finalised. Listening to the coolly efficient way he answered most of the practice questions, Lorinda could see how he came by his nickname of 'Mr Smooth'. He even managed to include a few complimentary plugs for the resort without seeming to labour the point in any way.

Her mother had often accused her of possessing a streak of devilment and it came to the fore now as, still playing the part of reporter, she asked, 'Rumour has it that you were married once, Race. Is this true?'

His eyebrow arched towards his hairline and his eyes flashed a warning. 'None of your damn business,' he growled.

'Is that a denial or a confirmation?' she persisted.

'That's enough, Lorinda. I think you're getting a little carried away.'

But he hadn't answered her question, a nagging voice inside told her. Like most people in the entertainment industry, she had heard the rumour, but since Race never mentioned it, she had supposed it be just that—a rumour. Now she was no longer so sure. His anger at the question had been genuine, she was certain, and his refusal to answer seemed even more damning. 'What will you say if the press ask you that question?' she queried.

'As you're my agent here, I should say it's your job to see that they don't,' he said in a tone of dismissal. He studied her keenly. 'Anyway, I don't think the press want an answer to that question as much as you do—am I right?'

'Of course not,' she denied, but her face flooded with colour. 'I was just walking you through the questions as you asked me to.'

'I'll bet you were,' he muttered.

She ignored this and stood up smoothly. 'I'll go and see that the conference room is ready.'

'Race Wolfendale, you are really something,' she thought grimly as she walked along the thatch-roofed walkway towards the main building. It seemed it was fine for him to probe her private feelings as long as she didn't trespass on his. Still, why should it matter to her whether he had been married or not? He was only a client, after all.

Nevertheless, her mind persisted in dwelling on the possibility as she went in search of Gerhardt Muller, who was supposed to have everything set up in accordance with the instructions she had telexed to him from Sydney.

Show business gossip had it that Race had married a chorus girl in Hollywood but had sought an annulment the next day when he discovered that his supposedly virgin bride had a child. Although no one had come up with any evidence to support the story, it persisted and was resurrected whenever the pictorial magazines were short of hard news. Since Race never confirmed or denied it, and the girl was never found, the story had assumed the quality of legend.

'Ah, good morning, Lorinda. I trust you slept well?'

'Good morning, Gerhardt. I was . . . very comfortable, thank you.' They went on to discuss the arrangements for the conference and Gerhardt proudly showed her the complicated sound recording system the hotel was equipped with. If needed, it could be adapted to translate a conference into several languages, although they would not be needing this facility today. After her guided tour, Lorinda agreed that the resort's array of video and projection equipment was the equal of any she had seen.

Gerhardt glowed with pride at her praise. 'We hope to attract international conferences to the island,' he told her, 'so we have equipped it as a convention centre as well as a resort.' He glanced at his watch. 'Chuck will be flying your guests in at any moment. Would you like me to go down to the helipad to welcome them?'

She smiled warmly. 'That would be a nice touch. I have to stay here in case Race needs anything—he'll be here in a few minutes.'

Ever punctual, he arrived just as Gerhardt was leaving for the helipad, and took in the room layout at a sweeping glance. 'You've done a good job here,' he told Lorinda.

'Try not to sound so surprised,' she murmured.

'What was that?'

'Oh, nothing.' She led him through to a back room where he could wait out of sight, ready to make a grand entrance when the media were assembled. She appraised him with a professional eye and was well pleased with his choice of French blue silk shirt left open to the chest, with front-pleated beige jeans. Luckily, he had an excellent skin and such an even tan that he wouldn't need any TV make-up at all. How many performers could say the same? she wondered, a little awed.

She left him relaxing in an armchair and returned to the main room where the first journalists were filing in. Some of them knew her and greeted her with a friendly, 'Hi, Lori, how's things?' She returned the greetings, trying to look coolly professional despite the nerves which were jumping in her stomach. Max's business depended on the success of this opening and it was all she could do not to cross her fingers as she sent up a silent prayer that all would go well. Occasionally she darted a nervous glance at the clock on the far wall. Where on earth was Simone Dyson—she should have been here by now.

'She was not on the first or second flights with the journalists,' Gerhardt told her in an undertone. 'I sent Chuck back to the airport in case she was delayed. If that was the case, he will have her here before the conference is concluded.'

'I hope she makes it,' Lorinda said into his ear. At least the star was here, that was the main thing. They could manage without Simone if they had to, but without Race—the prospect was unthinkable. She knew of situations where the guest of honour had simply failed to arrive, and it had been left to a hapless press agent to pacify a disappointed press corps. She hoped that would never happen to her.

At last they were all seated. She couldn't wait for Simone any longer, so she handed out the last of the press kits containing photos and background material on the stars and the resort, then took her place on the dais in front of a battery of microphones.

She leaned forward towards the mikes to introduce herself as Race's agent in Australia, and invited them to call on her to arrange features, exclusive interviews and guest appearances. There was a subdued buzz of talk, then silence, followed by applause when she said, 'Ladies and gentlemen, please welcome Race Wolfendale.'

He acknowledged the welcome with a wave as he strode from the anteroom across the floor to the microphones, where he made the expected speech about how glad he was to be in Australia and how disappointed he had been that there were no kangaroos in downtown Sydney. This brought some laughter and eased the tension in the room so that Lorinda began to relax slightly.

The friendly give-and-take between star and media continued for the rest of the morning as Race answered some questions fully and fielded those he felt unable to answer with polite evasions. Listening to him, Lorinda knew she was in the presence of a master. Even the cynics among the media seemed charmed by him.

A stir at the back of the room drew everyone's attention as the double doors were flung wide.

'So sorry I'm late, folks.'

She paused in the doorway just long enough for the photographers to record her entrance, then made her way slowly between the rows of seats to the front of the room.

Hardly pausing in his address, Race bent to offer her a hand on to the dais, then turned back to microphones. 'Some things are definitely better late than never,' he quipped, 'and may I introduce one of them—Miss Simone Dyson!'

This time the applause was accompanied by wolf whistles from the cameramen, and Simone blew them a kiss of appreciation. 'Thanks, darlings,' she said into the mike. 'My plane was delayed getting into Cairns—one of those typhoons or something,'

'Don't you mean tycoons?' one of the reporters catcalled.

She flashed him a smile. 'Think the worst, darling. The others know what a pure life I lead.'

Did she imagine it, or had Race's expression tightened fractionally at Simone's entrance? Maybe it was just his annoyance at her late arrival, but a sixth sense told Lorinda there was more to it than that. He had said he knew Simone well, but maybe he didn't like her very much.

To Lorinda's chagrin, she found this idea curiously satisfying. She had already taken a dislike to the dancer at first sight. There was something patently insincere about her, and she had no doubt the press were aware of it. From the backgrounders she had read, Lorinda knew Simone had even been known to throw furniture at reporters who antagonised her. But they endured her tantrums and notorious lateness because she was what they called 'good copy'. There was always a romance in the offing, usually with a prince, sheik or Hollywood mogul, and she took a great picture. As she moved around the stage now, Lorinda saw that the photographers were having a field day snapping her in various provocative poses. She doubted very much whether the dancer had just stepped off a plane dressed as she was in a Hawaiian printed sarong and very little else, with a hibiscus caught in her coal black waist-length hair, and a ton of make-up around her large alluring eyes.

Very little was known about Simone's past, and she encouraged speculation. Doubtless it was more colourful than the reality, Lorinda thought sourly, then chided herself. She didn't really know the woman well enough to be passing judgement.

Race was making wind-up signals to her under the table, but as she rose to end the conference, a man at the back of the hall jumped to his feet.

'Ted Coleby, *National Examiner*,' he stated. 'Tell me, Race, is it true that you have a wife and child you never see?'

Race's jaw tightened and he shot Lorinda a venomous look which was quickly masked by a professional smile. 'No, that is not true,' he said, 'and that's all we have time for today. Thank you all for coming, and good afternoon.'

There was a chorus of last-minute questions, but Race smilingly dismissed them as he strode towards the ante-room, followed by ·Simone. Lorinda quickly stepped across the doorway and reiterated that the conference was over. When this met with a disappointed murmur, she said cheerfully, 'You've all had your money's worth. The resort has laid on a buffet lunch and drinks in the Cowrie Room next door. Enjoy yourselves!'

There were a few half-hearted protests, but they all headed towards the main exit. Watching them go, she grinned wryly. It seemed even a group of hard-headed journalists could still be sidetracked by the idea of a free lunch, especially on the scale they could expect from a resort like Windi Bay.

When they had all gone, she closed the double doors and sagged against them, her smile abruptly vanishing. If only that reporter—what was his name? Coleby from the *Examiner*—hadn't asked about Race's marriage. Dear Lord! From his expression, he must think she had planted that question.

Anxiously she hurried towards the ante-room, not at all sure of her reception. Simone was languishing on a couch with a drink in one hand and a cigarette in the other, but Race was pacing up and down like a caged animal. He looked at her savagely as she came in. 'You had to have your pound of flesh, didn't you?'

'Look, I know you think I planted that last question, but I swear . . .'

'Save it,' he interrupted. 'You probably know the story anyway and just want the satisfaction of seeing me pilloried with it, so here it is. I *was* married once— to Simone!'

Simone gestured with her cigarette. 'It's true—Lorinda, wasn't it? And it didn't work out, for all the reasons the gossipmongers said it didn't. Satisfied now?' With that, she rose gracefully and headed for the door. 'See you kiddies later. I'm going to sleep off my jet-lag.' She blew Race a kiss and was gone.

Lorinda's mind was reeling. So it *was* true that he had been married, and there was a child involved, as Simone had just confirmed. 'I didn't know, honestly,' she breathed. 'And I had nothing to do with the reporter's question.'

'Well, you know now,' Race said curtly. 'You're one of only a half-dozen people in the world who do, so if the details are printed while I'm in Australia, I'll know just who leaked them, and by the time I finish spreading the story about your unreliability around the industry, your career as an agent will be finished before it's properly begun.'

Lorinda leaned weakly against a table, too shocked to think. The fact that Race was a valuable client paled as she took in what he was saying, and suddenly she saw red. 'Mr Wolfendale—you told me blackmail is an ugly word where you come from. Well, it's just as ugly here too. For the last time, I did not know of your . . . relationship . . . with Miss Dyson, and I had nothing to do with that reporter's question. Unless I have your full confidence, I can't continue as your agent, so I may as well fly home right now.'

As she turned to go, she heard a deep rumbling sound and spun around in astonishment, to see Race laughing at her. He spread his hands wide in a gesture of defeat. 'O.K., honey, have it your way. Nobody could protest *that* much and not be as innocent as she claims.'

'Then you believe me?'

'I believe you. It just seemed like too much of a

coincidence that the reporter should ask the same question you asked not an hour before.'

'Well, it *was* just coincidence,' she insisted.

He nodded. 'I accept that. And I apologise. But I'm not particularly proud of that part of my life and I resent it when people insist on dragging it up.'

'Very well, I accept your apology,' she agreed. 'At least now I understand why you were so reluctant to have Simone Dyson on the same bill with you.'

'When you wrote and told me her contract had been signed, I was furious,' he admitted, 'but by then it was too late. What I don't understand is why she was so anxious to come here. From what I read in the trades, she isn't short of work. I wonder what she's up to.'

Something in the way he said this made Lorinda acutely uneasy. She, too, had an intuitive feeling the woman was up to something, but she told herself it was none of her business and said with forced lightness, 'I'd better see that the media are enjoying their lunch.'

Race stood up and stretched luxuriously. 'As for me, I'm going to take a quick swim, then spend the afternoon rehearsing. Join me there when you've finished with our friends next door.'

It was phrased as an order, but his tone made it sound like an invitation. Lorinda didn't quite know why, but the idea of sitting in on his rehearsal sent waves of pleasure surging through her as she headed for the Cowrie Room.

CHAPTER FIVE

AFTER assuring herself that the journalists were having a good time, Lorinda escaped as quickly as she could, feeling that she needed time to think.

On the way back to her suite she told herself that Race's past was none of her business. No doubt he wanted to keep his brief marriage quiet because he didn't want to tarnish his nice-guy image. The idea that he would walk out on a woman just because she had a child wouldn't go down too well with his army of female fans. Was the child his? She dismissed the idea at once—in that event, she was sure he would have stood by Simone. No, it had to be his precious image he was concerned about. No doubt he had paid Simone to keep their secret all these years. Maybe she had come here because she wanted more money. Her manager had said it was because she preferred to work in the tropics and Max had been so thrilled to get her at a price within the budget that he hadn't probed any further. Now Lorinda thought she knew the reason.

By the time she reached her room the perspiration was running in rivulets down her back. On impulse, she stepped out of her crumpled dress and slipped into her crocheted bikini, then snatched up a towel and set off to locate the pool she had glimpsed earlier, between the main building and her suite.

It was empty, she saw with relief. She had been afraid Race might still be there, but it looked as though he had already gone to rehearsal. So she dived into the sparkling water and swam slowly up and down the length of the pool several times, then rolled

over and floated on her back while she sorted out her
tangled thoughts.

There was no reason why she should care about
Race's past, except that he did say he wanted to go
out with her, but he was free now so there was
nothing wrong in that. Still, she found the idea of
his brief marriage and its unhappy end disturbing
and gradually, she realised why. More and more,
Race fitted the mould into which experience told her
all entertainers were cast. Oh, he was better-looking
and more talented than most, but his past proved
that he was every bit as footloose and irresponsible
as . . . as her father. The gypsy's warning had been
very timely. Without it, she might have been
tempted to fall for Race and make her mother's
mistake all over again.

'That's all our pool needed—its own mermaid!' She
opened her eyes to see Gerhardt standing on the edge
of the pool. 'Hello there. You seem to be enjoying
yourself.'

'Mmm, it's glorious.' Then another possibility
occurred to her. 'I hope you don't mind, Gerhardt. I
mean, it's not reserved for guests or anything?'

'Of course not,' he laughed. 'Besides, the kind of
guests we cater for here wouldn't dream of getting
their designer swimsuits wet. For them, this pool is
something to be seen looking decorative around,
nothing more.'

All the same, Lorinda swam to the side and levered
herself up on to the quarry-tiled surround. Gerhardt
picked up her towel, but instead of handing it to her,
he draped it around her shoulders and began to dry
her. 'I can do that,' she said uncomfortably.

He continued the slow massaging movements. 'All
part of the service, my dear.' He swathed the huge
towel around her so she was cocooned in it. 'There,

now you are a captive audience. At least long enough so I can ask you to join me for dinner tonight.'

She hugged the towel closer around herself like a security blanket. She didn't care for the idea of another solitary meal alone in her room tonight, and the idea of dining with Race was equally disturbing, so she heard herself accepting Gerhardt's invitation.

He beamed with pleasure. 'Until tonight, then.'

He took a step away, then bent suddenly and picked something from the grass. 'Yours?' he asked, handing her a tiny jewelled watch.

'Yes, it is—I would have left it behind,' she said thankfully. The watch had been a gift from her mother and she would have hated to lose it. A glance at its face brought her to her senses. 'Oh Lord, the rehearsal!' she gasped, jumping to her feet.

'I was wondering when you'd get around to remembering me,' said a languid voice from the shelter of a grove of palms near the main entrance.

How long had he been standing there in the shadows? 'I'm sorry, I didn't realise I'd been here so long.'

He looked meaningfully at Gerhardt, who had paused at the sound of Race's voice. 'At least you weren't lonely.'

Lorinda was about to demand what business it was of his then remembered that she was, technically at least, in his employ. 'I said I'm sorry,' she said irritably. 'Just give me a minute to dress and I'll join you at rehearsal.'

'Perhaps I should be the one to apologise,' Gerhardt interrupted. 'I delayed Lorinda by inviting her to have dinner with me tonight.'

Race arched an ironic eyebrow. 'I see. She agreed, of course.'

Before he could say any more, Lorinda fled along

the path to her suite. She could almost hear what Race was thinking—she agreed, of course. Because Gerhardt was a gentleman to his boot-straps—middle-aged and as safe as any man she had ever gone out with, except Race Wolfendale. And her encounters with him had only convinced her that she was right in preferring friends to lovers. Somehow he always managed to upset her equilibrium as he aroused in her a whole new spectrum of feelings she preferred not to explore.

In her room, she showered and dressed hastily. It was really too hot to put her office dress back on again, so she slipped into a swirl-printed sundress with a halter neck which showed her smoothly tanned shoulders to advantage. Those of the media who were staying to cover the opening would have retired to their own rooms by now, so there was no reason why she shouldn't dress for comfort. Max had told her to treat this as a paid holiday—even though Race seemed to have overlooked that fact.

Her wet hair she wound into a chignon and slipped her feet into backless raffia sandals, then made haste for the Neptune Room, where Gerhardt had told her Race would be appearing.

The room was the resort's main restaurant and entertainment venue, and she caught her breath in amazement as she entered it. It was like descending beneath the sea. Everything was decorated in sea green and aqua, and fish swam lazily in giant tanks let into the walls. At the back of the room, waves cascaded soundlessly down one entire wall. At the moment in the half-light, the effect was cool and tranquil. At night, under artificial lighting, she imagined the effect would be sensational.

At the front of the room, Race was standing beside the piano where she could see him making notes on some sheets of music. At the sound of her footsteps on the parquet floor, he looked up. 'Can you play?'

Lorinda surveyed the gleaming grand piano, a far cry from the ancient iron-framed model she and her mother amused themselves playing at home. 'Passably. Why?'

'My musical director has gone to Cairns on an unexpected errand and won't be back until later today. Can you work with me until then?'

'Well, I'm not very good—but I'll try.'

'Good girl! Can you sight-read?'

For the first time, she thanked her stars for having a father in the entertainment business. Music had been a part of her life since she could walk. She nodded, and Race passed her the score he'd finished marking. 'Run through that for me.'

She sat down at the beautiful instrument and ran her fingers experimentally over the keys. Then she studied the sheet music for a few minutes and began to play as Race watched and listened critically. In her nervousness, she fluffed the first few bars, but he surprised her by saying nothing and waiting patiently until she got it right. She recognised the song—it was 'The Night, the Stars and You', which had earned Race a platinum record soon after he had recorded it.

Unexpectedly, he came in halfway and began to sing with her, adjusting himself easily to her inexpert timing. She looked up and he smiled encouragingly, sending a thrill of pleasure through her, although she reminded herself that the smile was only a part of his stage presentation. Still, when he sang '. . . I saw in your eyes, that sweet surprise, There was just the night, the stars and you', she had the uncanny feeling that he was singing to her alone. Then she told herself she was being foolish—that was exactly the impression he intended to create, and which had won him millions of adoring fans who all believed the same thing.

Despite her attempts to rationalise it, she was still affected by the sound of his velvety tenor voice, washing over her like a caress, as he sang the sweet loving words. 'Soon you'll be my wife, You've completed my life, There's the night and the stars and we two.'

The last notes died away and she sat where she was, her slender fingers still resting on the keys, achingly aware that he had moved around to her side of the piano during the song. He leaned across her to make a small adjustment to the score and his face came very close to hers. Lorinda held her breath, hardly daring to move until he moved away again. But instead he turned his head and suddenly his lips were on hers.

The promise of the song was fulfilled in that sweet, heady moment when all her sane sensible promises to herself were swept away on a tide of sheer longing. She felt his hands warm on her bare shoulders, then he drew her up from the piano stool and pulled her close to him so their bodies moulded into one line.

She was shaken by the strength of her own feelings which swept her along on a giant tidal wave. She was drowning, and what was worse, she didn't care, so long as this marvellous feeling never ended. Race didn't seem to be in any hurry either. His lips roved over her face like the fingers of a blind man, exploring the corners of her mouth, her brows and the hollow of her throat where a pulse beat like an imprisoned bird.

'Oh, Lorinda, I knew it could be like this!'

'Race I . . . we . . . we shouldn't.'

For answer, he claimed her mouth again with his own. 'Now tell me we shouldn't,' he murmured. To her horror, she felt her lips part unresistingly under his. No one had ever kissed her like that. Until this moment, she hadn't known such powerful sensations existed. She knew he could ask anything of her then and she would be powerless to resist.

Suddenly they were blinded by a brilliant flash of light which seemed even more penetrating in the gloom of the restaurant.

'What the hell . . .!' Race wrenched himself free from her.

'Thank you, folks. I can already see the caption—"star and agent make sweet music together"!'

In a daze, Lorinda took in what was going on. While they had been oblivious to everything but themselves, Ted Coleby from the *Examiner* had discovered them and snapped a picture of her in Race's arms.

'You wouldn't print that!' she gasped.

'Watch me, honey,' he told her happily, and backed quickly out of the room, as if afraid that Race would snatch the camera from him and destroy the film.

Lorinda turned to Race, whose mouth, so passionately soft a moment ago, was now set in a grim line. 'He means to print it, doesn't he?' she queried unhappily.

'Of course he does,' he said savagely.

She jumped back as if stung. 'What . . . I mean . . . will it harm your image?'

His eyes blazed. '*My* image? Dammit, woman, I was thinking about *your* image! The papers are always digging into my private life. I can handle it, but I'm not so sure you can.' He stalked across to the wall phone and pulled the handset roughly from the cradle, punching buttons with his other hand.

'What are you going to do?' she asked anxiously.

'I'm having Coleby thrown off the island!'

Her hand flew to her mouth. All Max's hard work promoting the resort would be ruined if the media turned against them, as they might if Race had one of their number thrown out. 'No, please, don't do that,' she begged. 'It will only make things worse. Maybe if we ignore it, it will all blow over.'

Race frowned. 'It might. On the other hand . . .' Still, he slowly replaced the receiver. 'Hell, Lorinda, I didn't mean to get you into a mess like this!'

She couldn't blame him entirely, for she had been more than willing to surrender to his advances, she could hardly deny that. 'It's all right really,' she said, striving to sound offhand.

'Then . . . just now . . . it didn't mean anything to you?'

'No!'

He regarded her for a long moment, his expression cold. Then he moved back to the piano and began methodically collecting his music together. She felt rooted to the spot, unable to move a muscle. When he had finished, he looked at her again with a curious half-smile. 'You're a damned liar, Lorinda.'

With a strangled cry she turned and ran from the room. His kiss didn't mean anything to her—it didn't, she told herself over and over. But his parting words echoed in her brain. 'You're a liar, Lorinda,' and in her heart she knew that she was. His kiss did do something to her—something so compellingly wonderful she was almost afraid to admit it even to herself.

In her headlong flight, she almost cannoned into Simone Dyson. The dancer was also apparently planning to rehearse, for she was dressed in scarlet tights and leotard, with a skimpy black rehearsal skirt tied around her hips. Her long black hair was plaited and coiled on top of her head.

'Where are you off to in such a panic?' she queried.

'I—er—I'm not feeling very well,' Lorinda improvised.

Simone composed her expression into one of

concern, but it did not reach her dark, flashing eyes. 'Poor dear,' she murmured. 'Maybe if you lie down you'll feel better, hmm?'

'Yes, I suppose so. Excuse me.' Lorinda all but pushed past the dancer and out of the lobby, but she could feel the woman's quizzical expression boring into her back as she went, then a moment later she heard Race's deep throaty laugh and Simone's high-pitched one coming from the Neptune Room.

By the time she reached her suite, she really *did* have a headache. Whether it was the tension of being in the same room with Race or the unaccustomed exposure to the tropical sun, she couldn't be sure, but the throbbing at her temples increased until she was forced to swallow some aspirin and draw the curtains to darken her room.

While she waited for the tablets to take effect she picked up the phone and dialled Gerhardt's extension. He sounded genuinely disappointed that she was not well enough to join him for dinner and offered to send the resort's nurse to see her.

'No, it's nothing serious, really,' she assured him. 'Just too much hot sun, that's all.'

'Let's hope that is all that's wrong,' he said worriedly. 'I'd like to call around later in the evening, just to check on you.'

'Thanks, but there's no need to worry, really.' She hoped he wouldn't come by later, she thought as she replaced the receiver and lay back against her pillows.

The tablets must have made her drowsy, because it was quite dark when she was awakened by a gentle tapping on her door. Groggily, she got up and without bothering to switch on a light, groped her way to the entrance hall.

Gerhardt was at the door. 'I just wanted to satisfy myself that you were all right.'

Lorinda smiled warmly. 'It's very kind of you. But sleep did the trick. As you can see, I'm fine now.'

'That is good news. Would you like me to have some supper sent up for you?'

'Please don't trouble. There's fruit and cheese in the refrigerator in my room—it's all I could manage, really.'

He appraised her slender figure silhouetted in the doorway. 'Fruit and cheese is not enough,' he said severely. 'However, I will not insist—this time. But I do not want you collapsing on me.'

'Understood,' she laughed. 'Goodnight, Gerhardt.'

Reluctantly, he left her and strode back towards the main building. Lorinda stayed where she was for the moment, savouring the refreshing feel of the perfumed night air. Here she was out of earshot of the Neptune Room where the orchestra would be playing for those guests who liked to dance the night away, and it was easy to imagine she was alone on this beautiful island.

A movement near Race's suite caught her eye. It was Simone. As she watched, the dancer came up the path from her own suite and tapped on Race's door. Lorinda knew she shouldn't stay, but if she moved, Simone would see her there and think she had been spying. So she stood rooted to the spot and watched in horrid fascination as Race's door opened. He said something to Simone, but too low for Lorinda to catch, then Simone put both arms around his neck and drew his head down to hers. Quickly he pulled her inside and closed the door.

Mechanically, Lorinda retreated into her own suite and shut her door. The marriage between Race and Simone might be over, but it was obvious there was still something between them. Angrily, she dashed the back of her hand over her lips as if to remove any lingering trace of his kiss this afternoon. Apparently she was just a stopgap until he could have the real object of his desires in his arms again.

More and more he was proving how right she was to guard her heart against men like him. They were all alike, fickle and irresponsible, and it would be some time before she allowed him to kiss her again.

So why did this thought make her feel so miserable? Why did her traitorous brain persist in replaying over and over the disturbing sensations his kiss had aroused? It was very late, but on impulse, she picked up the phone and asked to be connected to the convalescent home where her mother was staying. The thought that Race would be paying for the expensive interstate call gave her a little satisfaction at least.

But instead of making her feel better, the call only served to remind her how far apart she and her mother were. After a few minutes of desultory conversation during which she talked about everything except Race Wolfendale, Lorinda was almost glad to set the phone down again. Although she was delighted to hear her mother say she was making good progress, the call left her feeling emptier and more alone than ever.

Next morning she awoke with a vague feeling of unease. But it was only when the chambermaid delivered her breakfast tray and she caught sight of the folded newspaper lying on it that she remembered— the photo!

With shaking hands she unrolled the paper and spread it out on the bed. It was every bit as bad as she had expected. There, splashed across four columns, was the black and white shot of Race kissing her passionately, complete with Coleby's byline and 'sweet music' caption. His story speculated freely about the possibility of a love affair between star and agent in the romantic setting of Windi Bay. With a strangely detached sensation, she noted that the story was excellent publicity for the resort. Max would be pleased. But what would he think about the supposed romance between herself and Race? And what if her mother read the story?

She became aware that her heart was pounding in her breast. To calm herself, she picked up her brush and began methodically brushing her long hair. By the time she reached her usual hundred strokes she could at least view the picture more objectively. The *Examiner* was a daily newspaper, so it was likely that some other story would be front-page news tomorrow and she and Race would be forgotten. All they had to do until then was deny any truth in the story and the media would soon lose interest.

She had almost convinced herself that it would all blow over if only she was patient, when there was an unholy commotion at her door. It burst open and Simone Dyson hurtled into the room brandishing a copy which she thrust accusingly at Lorinda. 'Of all the underhanded schemers!' she raged. 'How do you explain *this*?'

The dancer's fury was so tangible that Lorinda backed away instinctively, but Simone followed her, waving the paper in her face. Her eyes were wild and her expression was twisted with a kind of madness which scared Lorinda.

'Simone . . . you know how the press distort things.'

'Distortion!' screeched Simone. 'You call this distortion? Next thing you'll be telling me they retouched the photo! Well, I've got news for you. Race Wolfendale is my property and I mean to have him back . . . and no two-bit agent is going to get in my way!' With that she launched herself at Lorinda and her long, scarlet-tipped nails raked the air inches from Lorinda's face.

Lorinda threw an arm up to shield her face and

gasped as the dancer's fingernails left a trail of marks across her forearm, drawing blood. Really frightened now, she backed on to the balcony, but Simone stalked her with a viciously determined look. She felt the balcony wall against her back and looked wildly around for a way of escape as Simone advanced on her. Then she screamed as the dancer grasped her long hair and twisted it savagely so her head was forced backwards and her body was bowed back across the wall. She struck out wildly with her hands, but they encountered empty air as Simone used her professional agility to twist herself out of reach.

Lorinda felt as though her back was breaking and just as she thought her hair would be torn out by its roots, Simone was wrenched away from her and thrown roughly across the balcony. There she stayed, spitting like a she-cat as Race helped a sobbing Lorinda into a chair.

'Simone, this time you've gone too far,' he said grimly.

'She attacked me—I had to defend myself,' she lied glibly.

Race's face twisted into a disbelieving sneer. 'Yeah, sure. Then why is Lorinda the one with your nail marks on her?' Tenderly he bound his handkerchief over the scratches and turned to Lorinda. 'Do you want to press charges?'

She looked up at him, too shocked by the last few minutes to comprehend what he was suggesting. 'Charges?'

'Assault—against Simone. You've got ample grounds.'

'But no witnesses,' muttered Simone. 'It's just her word again mine.'

'Shut up, you little cat,' he railed. 'Lorinda?'

Her head was spinning. If she charged Simone with

assault it would drag them all into a mire of statements to the police, court appearances and goodness knew what else. Since Race Wolfendale was involved the press would have a field day with the story. Added to which, Simone was right, there were no witnesses to prove that she had attacked Lorinda first. With her dazzling showgirl looks and provocative manner, she could probably twist the authorities around her little finger. 'No, I don't want to press charges,' she said at last.

'You're going to let her get away with this? Do you know what you're saying?'

Lorinda passed a tired hand over her eyes. 'I know what I'm doing. Believe me, it will be better for . . . for all of us, if nobody else knows.'

Simone was regarding her with smug satisfaction. She had been fairly sure this would be the outcome. But as she turned to leave, Race grabbed her roughly by the arm and spun her around. 'Don't think you're getting away with this,' he warned her. 'If you so much as come near Lorinda again, you'll have me to reckon with!'

'And what is she to you?' demanded Simone.

Race hesitated for the merest moment. 'Haven't you worked it out yet? Lorinda and I are going to be married.'

Simone gave them both such a venomous look that Lorinda flinched. 'A distortion of the press,' she sneered. 'So the story was true after all!'

'Yes, it's true. So now you see why you'd better not come near Lorinda again.'

'Oh, I see. I see a lot of things,' Simone said cryptically. 'And I guess I should say I'm sorry.'

Even Race looked surprised. 'That wouldn't hurt.'

'I'm sorry . . . that you got here before I had the chance to break her neck!' hissed Simone, and flounced out.

Race moved as if to go after her, but Lorinda restrained him. 'Please, no more unpleasantness,' she begged. 'I've caused enough trouble as it is.'

Tenderly Race pushed the perspiration-damp hair back from her forehead. '*You've* caused trouble! It looked to me as if Simone was doing that.'

'But the photo started it. I didn't realise that you two were still . . .'

'Still what?'

'Nothing.' There was no point in letting him think she had been spying on them last night. Besides, why give him the chance to deny it, which he probably would do? It seemed as if lies tripped very easily off his tongue. Which reminded her, 'Why did you tell her we were engaged?'

'Simone has a very violent temper, as you now realise. If I didn't give her an iron-clad reason to leave you alone, she might do some real harm. I know her well, and she tends to act first and think later.'

'I suppose I should be grateful,' Lorinda said tiredly. 'But it seems we've only got in deeper by telling her that. On top of the photo, everyone will believe there's something between us—and there isn't.'

'No,' Race admitted, 'but then no one knows about it but we three, so there's no harm done. And it did get you off the hook with Simone.'

But for how long? she wondered. She mustered a wan smile. 'Yes, it did for now, I suppose.'

'Friends, then?'

There was no point in making any more fuss. 'Friends.'

'That's the spirit!'

When he suggested she might try to eat some breakfast her stomach churned at the very idea and she shook her head. 'I couldn't eat a thing.'

'Well, how about joining me for a swim? You'll feel better for it, and the salt water's the best thing for those scratches.'

He gave her such a boyish look of appeal that she capitulated, conceding that a swim would be the best thing for her right now. Race waited while she changed into her bikini, then made her sit on his balcony while he got into his swim-shorts. She wondered if he was afraid to let her out of his sight in case Simone attacked her again.

They were ready at last, but surprisingly he didn't lead the way to the hotel pool. Instead, he turned down a path between groves of palm trees, to where the land reached out into the sea with two embracing arms, making a safe, inviting lagoon which was fringed with coral at the mouth, so the risk of sharks was minimal.

Enchanted, Lorinda paused at the edge of the beach. 'It's lovely—like a film set!'

'Isn't it! Come on, I'll race you out to the pontoon.'

The water was warm in the shallows and she could see tiny fish darting in and out between the rocks. Where the sand shelf dropped away it became abruptly colder, but she found the blue-green water bracing and it seemed to wash away the unpleasantness of the morning. Race swam strongly ahead of her, cutting through the water like a shark. She despaired of keeping up with him and swam at her own unhurried pace, arriving some time after him at the pontoon moored in the middle of the lagoon.

He helped her up on to the bobbing surface and they stretched full length on it to soak up the sun which was not yet too fierce, as it would be later in the day.

The warmth and gentle rocking motion lulled her into a pleasant somnolence, but just when she was dozing off completely, the sound of voices carrying from the shore disturbed her. Curiously, she sat up and started as she looked shorewards. Race was asleep beside her and she nudged his shoulder. 'Race, look!'

He sat up slowly and looked where she indicated. On the beach, a knot of people was gathered where they had left their towels.

'You don't suppose they think we're in trouble, do you?'

Race frowned. 'No. They can see us perfectly well from here.' Suddenly he swore under his breath. 'I think we'd better get back to the beach!'

Baffled, Lorinda followed him into the water and they swam side by side until they could stand up in the shallows. From here, she recognised the people waiting for them as the journalists who were staying to cover the resort opening. As soon as Race and Lorinda came up on to the beach their cameras began clicking and they were immediately surrounded.

'Congratulations, you two!'

'How long have you known Miss Fleming, Race?'

'When's the happy day?'

Race held up a hand for silence. 'May I ask how you found out?'

Ted Coleby spoke up. 'Miss Dyson broke the news to us after breakfast. I knew that photo was a scoop!'

Simone! 'Why, that little . . .' Then he remembered that the journalists were hanging on to his every word. Lorinda looked at him beseechingly, but he shrugged. 'Simone was telling you what we told her this morning,' he said carefully. 'And since we haven't set a date or any other details yet, that's all I can say for the moment.'

With the press tagging along like hounds in full cry, he took Lorinda's hand and hurried her up the path back to the hotel. Only when they were safely back in

her suite did Lorinda allow herself to consider the full
import of what had just happened.

'Why didn't you tell them the truth?' she asked
Race.

He rummaged in her refrigerator and came up with
two miniature bottles of brandy which he poured over
ice, adding dry ginger ale and handing her one before
he answered. 'That's exactly what she's hoping we'll
do. This is the only way to convince her that you
really are under my protection. Now she'll have to
believe that we're engaged.'

She took a gulp of her drink and felt the fiery liquid
burn her throat, but its effect was bracing. 'But the
whole world will believe we're engaged, or they will as
soon as the wire services have a chance to phone in the
story.' She glanced at her watch lying on the bedside
table. 'It'll make the evening editions, then what will I
do?'

'You seem to forget that I'm in this as deeply as you
are.'

It was on the tip of her tongue to remind him that
he was always being paired off with some eligible
starlet or other. This whole experience was bewilder-
ingly new to her. He seemed to sense her dismay, for
he sat down on the bed beside her. 'Is it so bad, the
idea of being engaged to me?'

How could she tell him that she was alarmed
beyond belief at the speed with which events were
overtaking her? The gypsy's warning was no longer a
joke—it was close to becoming a reality. Race was a
tall dark stranger and he had already usurped her
peace of mind, and . . . now this! What else would he
take from her before this was over?

All her careful plans to avoid emotional entanglements had been to no avail. She was trapped in an
engagement only she knew to be false. Would she be

forced to marry him next? She had an irrational urge to giggle and knew she was verging on hysteria. 'I need some time to get used to the idea,' she said at last. 'This morning has been more than I can handle, so I'd like to lie down for a while. With the opening tonight, it's going to be a long day, and the way I feel right now, I might not survive it.'

But the worst was still to come. After checking with Gerhardt that all the arrangements were in hand for tonight's opening, Lorinda lay down on her bed and tried to bring some order to her confused thoughts. Engaged to Race Wolfendale ... engaged to Race Wolfendale ... the idea went around and around her exhausted brain like a litany. She wasn't aware that she had fallen asleep until she was awakened by the shrilling of the phone on her bedside table. Still half asleep, she groped for it and was startled into full wakefulness by the sound of Max's voice. 'Max! It's good to hear from you.' Then panic gripped her. 'Mum, is she ...'

'She's fine,' he assured her at once. 'In fact I'm at the nursing home with her right now. We're both delighted for you, Lori. I'll put Arna on.'

Before she could sort out what he meant by this, her mother's voice came on the line. 'Darling, I'm so happy for you! Race is a wonderful man and I'm sure he'll make you very happy.'

'Race? But ...' Then the morning's events came flooding back. They were supposed to be engaged. 'But how did you find out so quickly?'

'It was on the radio, darling. They're calling it the romance of the year!'

Then Max came back on the line. 'Your mother's getting over-excited,' he explained. 'Her doctor has told her to take things easy, but this news of yours has been like a tonic to her. I wish you could see how good she's been looking ever since she heard the announcement!'

Lorinda tried to interrupt Max to tell him the truth, then the full impact of what he was saying overwhelmed her. How could she risk her mother's hard-won health by telling them what had happened? Distantly she heard herself accepting Max's congratulations and best wishes for the opening, and replaced the receiver.

It seemed she would have to carry on with the fiction of an engagement to Race, at least until her mother was recovered enough to cope with the truth. She shivered as she had a mental vision of the gypsy making her dire prediction. How she would laugh now if she knew how much havoc her tall dark stranger was causing in Lorinda's life!

She showered, standing for a long time under the icy jets to see if she could wake herself up—she had to be dreaming. But by the time she emerged from the shower she knew she was wide awake and the engagement was real enough. What was she going to do? In a daze, she began to dress for the opening.

CHAPTER SIX

As soon as she walked into the Neptune Room Lorinda was glad Race had made her bring her own dress for the opening. She would have died of shame if she had been forced through her own foolishness to face all these fabulously dressed people in her mother's skirt and blouse. As it was, she felt that her home-made evening gown was no match for the designer clothes the other women were wearing. She was totally unaware of the enchanting picture she presented. The simple lines of the strapless gown suited her to perfection and skimmed the slender contours of her body with becoming grace. Her hours in the sun had made the highlights in her hair more noticeable than usual so that tonight, her cornsilk-coloured locks seemed shot through with gold.

Admiring glances followed her progress through the lobby and Gerhardt Muller came hurrying up as she entered the restaurant. He took her hand and pressed it to his lips in the timeless continental gesture. 'Lorinda, words cannot describe how lovely you look!'

'Thank you, Gerhardt. Flattery is good for a woman's soul, even if it isn't true.'

'Oh, but it is in your case.' He took her arm possessively. 'Come, you will do me the honour of sharing my table, I hope?'

'Thank you—I'd like that.' She was relieved to have his company for the evening. Race was too busy preparing for the opening to pay her any attention and he had refused her offer to assist backstage. She tried to tell herself it didn't matter, but she still felt a twinge

of something alarmingly like jealousy as she thought of
how Simone had dismissed her, saying they needed to
be alone before the performance. She looked up as a
waiter arrived and poured champagne for them.

Gerhardt lifted his glass to her. 'A toast to you and
Race,' he offered. 'May you have every happiness.'

'Thank you, you're very kind,' she murmured,
hating herself for misleading him. She took a sip from
her own glass. 'To the success of Windi Bay,' she
returned, then looked around at the glittering
company, 'not that there's any doubt of it!'

'Bookings for the future are already heavy,' he
confirmed. 'It seems the Barrier Reef was in need of
just such an exclusive resort. But you are changing the
subject. I was congratulating you and Race. Now I
understand why he was so angry with me for inviting
you out to dinner. It was naughty of you to let me
think there was any hope for me.'

Impulsively she covered his hand with hers. 'It
wasn't like that. Race and I . . . we . . . that is, I hadn't
decided anything until this morning.'

'I see. Then it was love at first sight—very
romantic.' He looked studiously down at the tablecloth.
'Forgive me, Lorinda, it is none of my business—but
you see, I could care for you very much if things were
different. I do not want to see you get hurt. You . . .
have the look of a woman in love. As for Race—I do
not know. But I am worried about the Dyson woman.
I have noticed how angry she looks when you are with
Race, and I think she means to make trouble.'

'It's all right, Gerhardt, and it's kind of you to be so
concerned, but there's nothing to worry about,' she
told him, trying to put conviction into her voice. 'I
know Simone doesn't like me, but Race will make sure
she behaves.' Which was true enough, she reflected. It
was for that reason Race had announced their

engagement, hoping it would be enough to make Simone leave her in peace.

However, she feared it had created the opposite effect. Whatever plan had made Simone so keen to come here had obviously included Race Wolfendale. 'He's mine,' Simone had said in a way which warned Lorinda that Simone's plans did not include his being engaged to someone else. She shivered slightly, although the night was warm, then looked around the brightly lit room for reassurance. Surely there was nothing Simone could do to harm her here?

She was distracted by the arrival of a waiter with the first course, and to her astonishment she realised she was hungry for the first time since she arrived.

The menu promised olive mistes, a chilled consommé, coral trout grilled in brown butter for the fish course and stuffed mushrooms as an entrée. Then there was a choice of entrecôte steak or roast Norfolk turkey with apple seasoning, served with dauphine potatoes and lima beans, steamed rice and a side salad.

After finishing most of her main course she had to decline dessert—a choice between orange cream pie and apricot melba. 'I shall go home pounds heavier!' she protested when Gerhardt tried to coax her to sample the apricot melba.

'Nonsense. This is the first substantial meal I've seen you take since you came, and I'm delighted you find it pleasing.' Over her protests he refilled her champagne glass.

She sipped the drink slowly, not wanting it to go to her head. 'What time does the show begin?'

Gerhardt glanced at his watch. 'In a few minutes. First, I will introduce the State Governor who will officially open the resort. Then Simone will dance for us, and after a short interval, it is Race's turn. After that the orchestra will play on until the last dancer has had enough.' He rose and leaned across to pat her hand. 'Relax, little one. All will be well, you'll see.'

As he walked towards the microphone, Lorinda suppressed a feeling of surprise. She was horribly tense, but hadn't known how much it showed. No matter how she told herself that her concern was purely professional, just part of her job, she knew it was more than that. Gerhardt said she had the look of a woman in love, but that was impossible, of course. He was a romantic at heart and no doubt liked to think she felt that way because of her supposed engagement. For whatever reason—and she shied away from examining her motives too closely—she wanted Race to be a huge success tonight.

She was so keyed up waiting for him to appear that she hardly heard the Governor's speech. She had been introduced to him formally earlier in the evening and she was dimly aware that he welcomed the resort's contribution to the state economy and said his government was delighted it had been established here. When he unveiled a plaque commemorating the occasion, she applauded with everyone else, but inwardly she was willing the first half of the evening to be over. But there was still Simone's appearance before the interval.

After the attack this morning she was surprised to find she enjoyed the dancer's performance. In spite of herself, she was forced to admit that Simone was very good. The restaurant lights were dimmed and only a single spotlight followed her across the stage. Abruptly it went out and there were gasps as the room was plunged into blackness. Then a torch flared in the darkness and Simone danced by its flickering light to the throb of jungle drums. It was as primitive and compelling as a native ritual, and the audience was entranced as she passed the flames over her arms and scantily clad body without apparent harm.

Then the tempo of the music changed. To the hypnotic piping of flutes, Simone glided on to the stage carrying a large wicker basket. Gracefully she set it down, then lifted its lid and threw it discus-style across the heads of the audience to a waiting stage hand. Every move was smoothly rehearsed. Then the gasps of admiration changed to a murmur of fear as she drew out of the basket a huge carpet snake which she proceeded to twine around her body.

'She does that rather well, don't you think?' Gerhardt said into her ear as the dance continued.

'Yes, she's very good,' Lorinda whispered back.

Gerhardt's gaze flickered over the audience watching in horrid fascination. 'I think our guests do not like her pet so much, though!'

Studying the nervous faces around her, Lorinda had to agree with them. She harboured a fear of snakes and Gerhardt's table brought them much too close to the creature for her comfort. Even though she had been told that Simone's 'pet' was quite harmless, the snake's long sinuous body and flickering tongue filled her with terror. She was relieved when the dance ended and the snake was fed back into its basket and carried offstage. The audience reaction was enthusiastic and Simone took several curtain calls before the applause died away. At the last one, Lorinda was surprised to see a look of something very like pain in the dancer's expression. It was there only fleetingly and was quickly masked by a professional smile, making Lorinda wonder if she had imagined it.

When the room lights came on again, waiters moved swiftly among the tables to serve coffee, liqueurs and mints. 'Cognac?' Gerhardt queried.

She was about to refuse, already feeling the heady

effects of the champagne, but the tight knot of nerves
in her stomach made the brandy seem like a good idea.
It would help her to relax before Race's performance.
It was foolish to worry, she knew. He was one of the
world's most successful entertainers both on stage and
in films. All his records had become hits and had
caused lesser talents to mutter about 'Wolfendale
clones', each following a different career with identical
flair. The fact remained that he was extraordinarily
successful, first in the musical field, then as a serious
actor. Part of it was sheer talent, but the rest was hard
work and dedication, Lorinda knew. Nevertheless,
when the lights went down she took a quick gulp of
her cognac. It was all she could do not to cross her
fingers.

The orchestra swung into Race's signature tune, the
title song from his film, *Beloved Stranger*, and he
strolled on to the stage looking totally at ease and
stunningly attractive.

Lorinda's heart constricted at the sight of him
standing alone in a pool of light, surrounded by
blackness. Beloved stranger—it was just how he
looked, she thought dreamily, then realised what she
was thinking. The brandy and champagne were
affecting her more than she allowed! He *was* a
stranger, but hardly a beloved one to her. He was the
tall dark stranger the gypsy had warned her about, and
she would do well to remember that their supposed
engagement was only a sham, lest the 'something of
value' the gypsy predicted he would take from her
ended up being her heart.

Still, she was disturbed by the intensity of her
reaction as she watched him on stage. He was
immaculately dressed in white figure-hugging trousers
and his white silk shirt edged with black was slashed
to the waist, allowing a glimpse of a heavy gold

medallion that glinted against his tanned skin as he
moved. He looked like a modern-day pirate, Lorinda
mused. It wasn't hard to imagine him swinging down
from the rigging of a tall-masted ship and sweeping
her into his arms. Then she nearly laughed aloud at
the fantastic direction her thoughts were taking. Pirate
indeed! She had better not have any more of the
excellent cognac if that was the result! With an effort,
she concentrated on his song, which was moving
towards the finale. She felt as if she would choke with
emotion when he sang the last words, 'Beloved, yes,
but stranger no more.' It was a beautiful song and he
sang it wonderfully well.

With the rest of the audience, she got to her feet,
clapping enthusiastically. A number of patrons called
'More, more!' and she was glad Race had rehearsed
several other songs in case he needed an encore. Now
he signalled to the orchestra and they began to play. A
chill ran down her spine as she recognised the opening
bars of 'The Night, the Stars and You.' It was *her*
song. Not that she had any special claim to it, of
course, but she *had* accompanied him when he
rehearsed this particular number . . . and then, he had
kissed her and she blushed as she recalled her own
uninhibited response.

As she looked up her eyes met Race's and something
in his expression told her he was remembering too.
What was he thinking now, as he sang the words
again? Was his body throbbing with remembered
sensation, as hers was, to her eternal shame . . . or was
he furious that his impulsive action had forced them to
pretend to be engaged?

A moment later she was unexpectedly bathed in the
rosy glow of a spotlight, and the audience broke into
applause when they recognised Race's 'fiancée'. She
tried to smile in acknowledgement, but inwardly she

was fuming. What on earth did Race think he was up to? The more fuss they made about their supposed engagement, the harder it would be to break it off later, when her mother was well enough to be told the truth.

But Race didn't seem to share her concern. He moved towards her and leaned against her table, and this time there was no doubt that he was singing to her. 'I saw in your eyes that sweet surprise—there was just the night, the stars and you.' Thinking that she would kill him for this later, she tried to meet his gaze squarely but was forced to turn away, disturbed by the powerful emotions she saw there. He was looking at her with such undisguised desire that she was shaken. It couldn't be real, it was just part of his act, she told herself over and over—yet, when he looked at her like that, something melted inside her. They were the only two people in the room and no one and nothing else mattered.

Around them, the applause swelled to a crescendo as Race reached the closing line, 'Soon you'll be my wife, you've completed my life, There's just the night, the stars and we two.' So help her, she was close to believing he meant it, and she found herself smiling back, her cheeks tinged with pink as much from the fire he was kindling inside her as from the rosy hue of the lighting. When Race reached for her hand and pressed it to his lips the audience signalled its approval. Embarrassed, Lorinda tried to pull free, but his grip tightened and he drew her to her feet to share the applause with him.

Then it was over. Like someone waking from a dream, Lorinda sank back into her seat as the room lights brightened again and Race disappeared back-stage. Automatically, she smiled and responded to the well-wishers who immediately crowded around the table to congratulate her and Race, but her mind persisted in dwelling on the last few minutes. It was crazy to read so much into what was only a polished performance, she knew, and yet had it all been an act? She was no longer so certain.

Gerhardt smiled at her across the table. 'That was very moving. It seems everyone wants to wish you and Race well tonight.'

Yes, it looked that way—until she glanced across the room to see Simone sitting in solitary splendour at a table near the orchestra, making no move to come over. She had changed out of her dance costume into a skin-tight pink sheath which made her body seem as snake-like as the creature she had danced with earlier. She was taking generous sips from a tall glass and her eyes met Lorinda's across the rim. Her expression was filled with hatred and . . . something else, dangerously like triumph. What had she been up to? Lorinda wondered, shaken. Gerhardt had been afraid that Simone might make trouble for her over the engagement, and, looking at her malevolent expression, Lorinda was suddenly afraid, too. If only they had never started this whole charade! Then she told herself she was being childish. What could Simone possibly do to her here?

Still, the dancer's triumphant expression haunted her as she walked back under the thatched roof to her own suite, so she jumped when a hand touched her elbow.

'Hey, I didn't meant to scare you!'

'Race! I'm so glad it's you.'

He turned her gently to face him. 'Honey, you're shaking—whatever is the matter?'

She couldn't very well tell him about the threat she had read in Simone's expression, or the disturbing way her female intuition was working overtime. So she smiled wanly, 'I'm O.K., just a little tired, that's all.'

He nodded understandingly. 'It has been rather a long day. You'd better get some rest—I don't want my future bride collapsing from exhaustion!'

She shivered again. 'I wish you wouldn't keep going on about us being engaged. It's not as if it was a real engagement, after all.'

'It was for your protection, Lori,' he reminded her a little stiffly.

'I know, for my mother's sake and to keep Simone in line,' she sighed. 'But it may have had the opposite effect.'

'What do you mean?' he demanded sharply.

She cast around for a way to put her fears into words. 'After you sang that song to me tonight, I saw her looking at me . . .'

'And?' he prompted.

'That's just it—I don't know. It's as if she was . . . pleased with herself about something. I had the feeling if I knew what it was, I wouldn't like it.'

Race put a comforting arm around her shoulders and she stiffened, unbearably conscious of the warmth of his skin against hers. 'I won't say you were imagining things, because I know Simone—but she also knows what I'll do to her if she tries anything. She'd probably been drinking and decided to show you her claws. Tomorrow we'll fly over to the mainland and choose an engagement ring for you. When she sees my ring on your finger, that ought to convince her to leave you alone.'

'Oh, but you don't have to do that!' she protested.

'Yes, I do. Our engagement won't be very convincing without a ring—Simone would soon smell a rat, and if the press start speculating about it your mother could hear about it.'

So it was for appearances' sake, not because he wanted her to wear his ring, Lorinda thought dejectedly, then chided herself for thinking like that when he was being so thoughtful.

Her disappointment must have showed on her face, because Race cupped her chin in his hand and tilted her face up to his. 'Aren't you pleased about the idea of choosing a ring? Most girls would be jumping up and down with excitement.'

With an effort, she stopped her jaw trembling at his touch, although she was sure he must feel the frantic beat of the pulse at her throat. 'I'm not most girls, am I? As far as I'm concerned, the ring will be on loan until we can get out of this sham engagement. It's not as if it means anything, is it?'

His voice was strained as he released her. 'No, of course not. Goodnight, Lorinda, sleep well.'

She knew there was little chance of that, as she bade him goodnight and closed the door of her suite. Despite his assurance that Simone was only 'showing her claws' as he put it, she felt distinctly uneasy. Still, she was comforted by the thought that Race's suite was only next door. If she needed anything, he wasn't far away.

'Stop it!' she told herself angrily, alarmed at the way her imagination insisted on making something out of nothing. Determinedly she took deep breaths of the clean sea air blowing in through the open balcony door, and told herself that Race was right, Simone was just bluffing.

In an attempt to allay her fears once and for all before she went to sleep, she stayed under the shower for ages, starting with the water as hot as she could bear, then toning it down to an icy blast that left her skin tingling. She felt better by the time she swathed herself in her terry-towelling robe and reached for her hair brush.

The ritual one hundred strokes did its usual job of

soothing and calming her, and as she pulled the brush through her long hair, she reflected on Race's strange attitude tonight. It was almost as if he enjoyed being engaged to her—which was insane, since he could have his pick of any woman that he wanted. So why did he go out of his way to emphasise their relationship to the world, by literally turning the spotlight on to them while he sang a blatant love song to her? It had to be his precious image again, nothing else made sense. For if it wasn't intended to show the world that this engagement was his idea then there was only one other possible explanation—he really cared for her. He mustn't, she told herself in anguish. No good could come of that, only the heartache that she knew followed every close relationship in her life when it inevitably had to end. No, he mustn't care for her— and she must not fall in love with him, at all costs. She already knew him well enough to know that if she ever entrusted her heart to anyone, it would be a man like Race—which was all the more reason not to take the risk.

Miserably, she wished again that they had never got involved in this crazy charade. If only she had never agreed to come to the island with him then she would not have had to take such terrible risks with her affections. For it *was* a risk, she acknowledged. The longer she was forced to act the part of Race's fiancée, the more she became aware of how much she could care for him if she gave herself the chance.

With a sigh, she set the brush down on her bedside table and flicked off the light, then shrugged out of her robe. Since she had come to the island, she had given up wearing a nightdress. Even with the resort's powerful air-conditioning system, she found it much easier to sleep with just her bare skin against the cool sheets. She had never even unfolded the down comforter which lay across the foot of the bed.

She climbed into the big bed, only now admitting how much the day had taken out of her emotionally. Blissfully, she stretched full length under the coverlet and closed her eyes, only to open them wide again in horror as she felt something move under the folds of the comforter at the foot of her bed.

Her breath came in a strangled rasp that rattled from between clenched lips as she felt the warm, dry thing slide against her bare legs. 'Oh God, it can't be!' The thing wound nerve-shatteringly slowly up the length of her body while she lay rigid, paralysed with fear. Her heart was pounding so rapidly, she felt as if it would burst from her chest. Then, mercifully, the snake emerged on the side of the bed farthest from her and began to inch its way down the coverlet towards the foot of the bed. Only when it was well clear of her, did she find the courage to heave the covers away with a mighty effort which drained her of strength. As she heard the thing thud on to the tiled floor, she heard a distant sound which began as a kitten's mew, then became a bloodcurdling scream. When she heard Race rattle the door handle and call to her, she realised the sound came from her own throat. He must have put his shoulder to the door, because there came the sound of wood splintering then he burst into the room.

'Lorinda, what in hell's name . . .'

As soon as he snapped on the light switch, he saw the snake, now coiled in the tumble of bedclothes on the floor. With a swift movement he spun the bedcover around it so the snake was caught in the folds, then carried it to the balcony where he dumped it on the tiles, then closed the connecting door so it was securely corralled.

At once he hurried to Lorinda's side and sat down

on the edge of the bed, gathering her into his arms. Gently he stroked her hair, which was damp with perspiration. 'Hush, honey! It's all right, it's outside now—you're safe.'

Still she couldn't stop shaking and her throat felt raw from her screams. 'I was so f-f-frightened,' she gasped. 'It was in my b-bed.' Her voice broke on a fresh wave of sobbing.

'My word, Lori, no wonder you're in such a state! Well, it's all right now, I'm here.'

He held her tightly until the sobs subsided and she began to stop trembling. Only then, as she clung to him, did she realise that she was totally naked in his arms. At once she squirmed away from him and looked frantically around for her robe.

'This what you're looking for?' he asked, handing her the garment. 'Relax, Lori, it's not as if I haven't seen a naked female before.'

She was about to retort that it was all very well for him, but no man had ever seen her like this before, then she remembered how quickly he had come to her aid. . This was no time to be worrying about appearances. Still, she felt an urgent need to get their relationship back on a less personal level. 'How ... how do you think it got in here?'

He glanced towards the balcony. 'Was the outside door open?'

Remembering how she had appreciated the cool sea breeze when she came in, she nodded.

'Then it must have escaped and come in here seeking a warm place to sleep.'

'It *is* Simone's snake, isn't it?'

His mouth was set in a grim line. 'Yes, it is.'

'Then you don't think she . . .'

'I don't know what I think,' he cut in sharply. 'But I mean to find out.'

Her face had gone white at the very idea that anyone could do such a horrible thing. Even though she knew the snake was harmless, the shock could well have been too much for her. But Race was right, there was no point in speculating about what could not be proved. The snake might well have simply escaped from its basket and come in here. Involuntarily, she shuddered.

Race saw the reaction and moved towards her. 'Will you be all right now?'

She tried to smile without much success. 'Yes, thanks. I doubt if I shall get much sleep, though, after . . . that.'

'Then I'll stay with you until you go to sleep. O.K.?'

She tried to protest that she would be all right, but in truth, she was comforted by the thought that he would be with her until she dropped off to sleep. For the first time, she noticed that his shirt was torn at the shoulder where he had burst open the door to reach her. 'Is your shoulder all right?' she asked anxiously.

He dismissed it with a wry grin. 'I'll have a nice bruise there in the morning, I guess. In Hollywood, we usually let the stuntmen do those scenes!'

Tenderly, Lorinda brushed his shoulder with her hand, slightly bemused that he had been willing to risk injury to himself for her. Unexpectedly, she began to giggle.

Race looked at her keenly. 'You're not going to get hysterical now, are you?'

'No, I was just wondering what Gerhardt will say about the door.'

'You really are an oddball female, you know that? I find you in bed with a snake and stark naked, and all you're worrying about is a damaged door!'

She blushed scarlet at the reminder of how he had found her. No man had ever seen her like that before.

Now she wondered what he was thinking as he gazed at her so strangely.

In the next moment, she had her answer when he pulled her close to him. 'Oh, Lori, you're so beautiful! When I saw you like that, I would have walked through brick walls to reach you if you needed me.'

Impatiently he pushed aside the shoulder of her gown and pressed his lips against the smooth skin of her shoulder. As she looked down at his bent head, she could smell the spicy tang of the hair groom he had used for the show earlier this evening and felt a strong impulse to run her fingers through the wavy mane. His breathing grew quicker and shallower as he traced a line of kisses across her shoulder and up the line of her jaw to her mouth, where he devoured it hungrily. Lorinda was all too conscious of the rising tide of his passion as his hands roved over her body under the towelling gown. His touch inflamed her senses in a way no one had ever done before and she was aware of a sensation like madness sweeping over her. She kissed him back with equal fervour and her arms came up to grip his shoulders and pull him even closer to her.

But when he tried to push her gently back against the pillows, a sudden rush of panic gripped her and she struggled to move away from him. 'No, Race, we . . . we mustn't!'

'Why not?' he breathed thickly, 'It's what we both want, isn't it? And we are engaged, after all.'

'No, it's not,' she protested, really frightened now. He was by far the stronger and could take her against her will if he chose. 'Our engagement's not real, remember?'

'But we could make it real, Lori. I care for you a lot, you know.'

No, he mustn't! Anything but that, she thought frantically. In a flash she realised what the 'something of value' that the gypsy predicted he would take from her might be. If she said yes to him now, and she had to admit that she was dangerously close to giving in, when he went away again— as everyone she had ever cared about went away—he would take her self-respect with him. She didn't think she could bear that. Even so, it was the hardest thing she had ever done to roll away from him and stand facing the bed, where he still lay looking up at her in puzzlement. 'What's the matter Lori? I was beginning to think you cared for me, too.'

'Well, I don't,' she retorted, hating herself for the lie. 'You're reading too much into this fake engagement business.'

His expression grew stony and the fire left his eyes at once. Slowly he stood up. 'I get the picture. I'm not old enough for you, is that it?'

She was genuinely baffled. 'I don't know what you mean.'

'Don't you?' he sneered. 'If I were old enough to be your father, would that do the trick, Lori?'

Old enough to be her father? What was that supposed to mean? Then it came back to her. Race thought she didn't want him to make love to her because she preferred older men—part of her father fixation, as he put it. How could she tell him it was because she had made a vow to herself never to share her heart with anyone because she was afraid to risk the pain of the inevitable parting? Perhaps it was better if he thought she had some sort of hang-up about her father. If she told him the truth, he would vow eternal love and promise never to leave her—but the day would come when he would go away just the same. But by then she would be hopelessly in love with him, and when he left she would have nothing— just like her mother, who had struggled to make a life for them after her father left, although she had been so tormented inside that she had never even taken a lover, far less contemplated marrying again. She didn't want that to happen to her, and she had already glimpsed enough of Race's character in his brief marriage and reported dalliances to know it was all too possible.

There was only one thing she could do. 'Perhaps you're right,' she said heavily. 'I need a father more than I need a lover.'

The look he gave her was cold and unyielding as he moved towards the door but he turned in the doorway. 'At least you have the guts to be honest,' he said bitterly. 'Prop a chair in front of this door. I'll have Gerhardt see to it in the morning.'

The broken door slammed against the frame and he was gone. She had achieved what she set out to do—deliberately invited the lesser pain of a quarrel now rather than risk heartbreak later, but knowing she had done the right thing didn't make it any easier to take. Was it possible she had already begun to care for Race past the point of no return? Oh Lord, she hoped not, because she had just burned her bridges beyond repair. She felt deathly weary and a look at her watch told her it was three in the morning, but not for anything would she sleep in that bed tonight. Feeling sure she wouldn't sleep a wink anyway, she dropped into one of the upholstered armchairs. Her head had barely touched the backrest when oblivion overcame her.

CHAPTER SEVEN

'OH, my goodness, whatever happened here, Miss Fleming?' Disorientated, Lorinda opened her eyes to find the maid standing in the centre of the room, holding her breakfast tray.

She stretched her cramped muscles. She must have fallen asleep in the chair after all. Seeing the maid's anxious face, she quickly reassured her that no one had tried to attack her during the night as the girl apparently thought. When Lorinda told her about the snake finding its way into her room, the maid turned pale and was only too happy to leave the tray inside, instead of taking it out to the balcony as she normally did.

'I'll have one of the gardeners remove it later,' she promised.

She tut-tutted a great deal over the splintered door but seemed impressed that Race had been so gallant. Another item for the Wolfendale legend, Lorinda thought sourly when the girl left.

Sleeping in such an uncomfortable position had left her feeling cramped and sore, and her mouth felt as if it was full of sawdust, so she was thankful that the tray held a glass of freshly squeezed orange juice which she drank at once. Then she poured herself a cup of steaming coffee and sipped it more slowly.

The morning sun streamed through the glass door leading to the balcony, but she did not dare to venture out to enjoy the morning air knowing that the snake was bound up in the bedclothes outside. She shuddered as she recalled the dry feel of it sliding up her legs—she doubted whether she would ever forget that terrifying moment. She was surprised that she had managed to sleep at all, far less as deeply as she had done, and that the experience hadn't haunted her dreams. Race had managed to blot out any such thoughts after he came to her rescue, and she bit her lip as she remembered how cold and distant he had looked when she rebuffed him. If only he knew what an effort that had cost her! He wasn't to know how sorely tempted she had been to let him stay—forever if he chose. No, he must never know that, she resolved firmly. Once she left this island, she would never see him again and it was up to her to put him out of her mind for good when the time came. For now, she would have to try not to be alone with him to avoid any chance of a repetition of last night.

One thing was certain, he wouldn't want to go through with his suggestion that they go to the mainland and choose an engagement ring. Perhaps he would even decide to call it off publicly. After last night there was no reason why he should care to protect her from Simone, or pander to her mother's ill health. Somehow the idea gave her no joy. Wistfully, she thought that it had been very pleasant being engaged to Race Wolfendale for a little while. Even if it was a pretence, she would have liked to go on pretending for just a little longer.

She sighed. This kind of thinking would get her nowhere; better to put her time to constructive use. In this frame of mind, she got out her writing things and composed a cheerful, chatty letter to her mother at the convalescent home. It was the first time she'd had an excuse to write to her mother and it was enjoyable, if a little strange. Of course, she couldn't be too honest about the situation between herself and Race, but she prepared her mother for the eventual announcement by saying that they wanted to make sure they were acting wisely before they made any firm wedding plans. Then she launched into an enthusiastic description of the resort and the opening night. The telephone was too limiting for long conversations over such a distance and she knew her mother would be eager to hear every scrap of information about the resort and the opening. By now she was probably bored with life at the convalescent home and anxious to get back to the flat, so the letter would cheer her up enormously.

Then she composed a shorter but equally chatty postcard to Marla at the office, and was just about to add a P.S. for Max when the phone by her bedside shrilled, startling her.

She hurried to pick it up. 'Max! How nice to hear your voice.'

'I wanted to congratulate you on your handling of the opening. It's already been on the morning news and at least one A.M. current affairs show.'

Lorinda was genuinely pleased. 'That's wonderful news! That means it should make the afternoon papers as well. Of course, the credit is due to Race—the audience loved him.'

'Don't be so modest,' Max returned. 'Your handling of the media has been first-rate throughout. I couldn't have done a better job myself. Of course, you getting engaged to the star didn't do the cause any harm, either.'

This was dangerous ground, and she cast about for a way to distract him from asking too many awkward questions. 'How's the rest of the tour looking?' she improvised.

'The Adelaide Festival Centre appearance is confirmed,' he told her. 'When Race returns to Sydney he'll be guest starring on the Dick Elder Show.'

'Max, how marvellous!' she breathed excitedly. Dick Elder had the top-rating talk show in the country and every agent in town wanted their clients to appear on it. It was a real feather in Max's cap to have pulled it off, but of course, even Dick Elder couldn't afford to ignore a star of Race's calibre.

'When is the last show scheduled?' he was asking.

'Tomorrow night. I'll fly home the next morning, as soon as Race leaves for Adelaide.' Why did that simple statement stab her like a physical pain? she wondered. She half-hoped Max would suggest she accompany Race to Adelaide, then she admitted to herself how dangerous that would be. The sooner she was out of his company, the better for her peace of mind.

'I wish I could spare you to go to Adelaide,' Max continued as if he had read her thoughts, 'but the Westsiders fly in at the end of the week and I'll need you to look after them. Twenty-five jazz musicians is more than I can handle on my own—even if they are the tops in their field.'

They exchanged a few more pleasantries and Max assured her that her mother was almost well enough to leave the convalescent home and return to her own flat. 'Her recovery dates almost from the day you announced your engagement,' he told her. 'She positively bloomed at the news, and after that it was progress all the way.'

Lorinda sighed heavily. Now was obviously not the right time to tell him the truth, just when her mother was doing so well. Perhaps it would be easier once they were together again in their own home. With a heavy heart, she said goodbye and replaced the receiver. Life went on, she reflected miserably. In two days Race would fly to Adelaide and she would return to Sydney to take up her next assignment, arranging the Australian tour of the famous jazz band. Just a couple of weeks earlier she would have been thrilled about the prospect. Now she knew it would be just a job to her, devoid of any special excitement, because the star was not Race Wolfendale.

Dejectedly, she sat down on the side of the bed and buried her face in both hands. Since there was no future in it, she might as well be honest with herself. She was head over heels in love with Race. The gypsy had been right. He had come into her life as a tall dark stranger and he had stolen her heart. What was she going to do? Even if he felt the same way, she knew what sort of life they would face together—the same one which made her mother so desperately unhappy. Race was an entertainer, like her father, and like him, would not be content with one woman for very long. Then she would have to put up with the gossip, the knowing looks and worst of all, the sympathy of friends and acquaintances. She would have to endure the long nights alone, never sure just where Race was or what he was doing. Then would come the day when he left for good. No, she couldn't go through that.

She was faced with the same choice surgeons had to make when an otherwise healthy patient was threatened by an infected limb. Their answer was usually to cut off the limb before it killed the rest of the patient. Well, she would have to be her own surgeon, and cut Race out of her life before he took over every part of it and her. Easier said than done, she reflected despondently. If the very thought of watching him fly away from her caused her such mental anguish, what would the reality be like?

Impulsively, she jumped to her feet. Dwelling on the situation was not going to change anything. Perhaps some physical activity would help take her mind off things. Since there was nothing for her to do until this evening's show, she decided to swim a few lengths of the hotel pool.

It took her only a few minutes to slip into her white crocheted bikini and snatch up a towel, then she headed next door to Race's suite to tell him where she would be. After last night, she was fairly sure he wouldn't want to go shopping for an engagement ring, but he might have some other plans, and since she was supposed to be his assistant, she owed him the courtesy of checking with him before she went off on her own pursuits.

There was no answer when she knocked on his door, but it was unlocked, so timidly she pushed it open.

'Race? Are you there?'

He was probably jogging on the beach again, she guessed, and went through the suite to the balcony to see if she could spot him on the sands. The silver expanse was empty of all but a couple of early morning sun-worshippers, so she turned back inside. Idly, she noted that his bed was made up in the almost military way Susie usually made them, but it was too early for the rooms to have been cleaned. It looked more as if the room had not been used at all last night.

Which was none of her business, she told herself sternly as she stepped outside again and pulled the door shut behind her. She almost bumped into Race, emerging from Simone's room, and he steadied her in a move which reminded her of that first time in the corridor outside the office. He took in her swimsuit and towel at a glance. 'Where do you think you're off to?'

'That's what I came to tell you. I'm going down to the pool, unless of course you need me for anything else.'

His expression softened and she thought he was about to make some teasing remark, then his jaw tightened and the cold look returned. 'I did have something else in mind, as it happens. Chuck is waiting to fly us to the mainland—we were going to buy a ring, remember?'

'Oh! But I thought . . . after last night . . .'

'What has last night got to do with it?' he asked evenly. 'The reason for the ring, as I recall, was to shore up the pretence of our engagement for your mother's sake.'

Lorinda noticed he made no mention of Simone this time. Perhaps he had already told her the truth and was only waiting until her mother was well enough, to call the whole thing off. His bed didn't look as if it had been slept in and he had emerged from Simone's room, which added up to only one thing—they had spent last night together. Simone had apparently given Race what Lorinda would not, so he had turned to the dancer after Lorinda had rebuffed him. She might be naïve, but she understood that men had needs of their own, and no doubt Simone was adept at satisfying them.

She should be feeling pleased with herself, she reflected. She had obviously reached the right conclusions about Race—he was every bit as irresponsible and fickle as her father. So why did she feel so utterly miserable at the idea of him spending the night with Simone?

'Well, are you going to get changed or are you planning to go shopping in that?' he demanded impatiently.

'I'm not going,' she said quietly.

His eyes blazed and she saw his fists clench as he fought for control. 'You're coming,' he said with deceptive softness. 'Part of your job is doing my bidding and I happen to want you with me today. Is that clear?'

It was on the tip of her tongue to remind him that he had threatened to ruin her career once before and she had called his bluff, then she thought better of it. There was no point in making trouble for Max just when everything was going so well—for the agency, at least. If she could just survive the next couple of days he would be gone from her life for good. She gave a mock salute. 'Yes, sir, Mr Wolfendale,' she said grimly, and turned on her heel.

Her childish gesture of slamming her door in his face proved futile when the door merely bounced off its splintered frame, an all too painful reminder of last night's events. Through the half-open door she could see Race leaning nonchalantly against the doorframe and she knew he was watching her under the half-closed lids.

Pointedly she snatched up the first skirt and blouse she came to in her wardrobe and slipped into the bathroom, sending the bolt home with a decisive click that she hoped he heard. Since she already had ample proof that he was capable of breaking a door down, she put little faith in the flimsy bolt and wasted no time getting out of the bikini and into the white linen skirt and green figured blouse. It was cut lower than she cared for, with a deep ruffle around the shoulders, giving it a gypsy air that she usually liked. Today, however, it seemed a touch too provocative, but not for anything was she going to go into the main room and choose another outfit under Race's mocking eye.

Her long hair she plaited and coiled on top of her head for coolness. A pair of hoop earings and white sling-back sandals completed the outfit. It was much too hot for make-up, so she settled for a film of moisturiser and a dash of natural-toned lipstick.

Emerging into the bedroom, she picked up her handbag and returned to Race, still standing in the doorway. 'Is this more to your liking, sir?' she asked defiantly.

His glance took in the low cut of the blouse and the bare expanse of tanned shoulder it revealed, then travelled down to the slender line of her skirt with its side split. 'You do believe in playing with fire, don't you?'

'If you'd rather I changed into something more businesslike . . .'

'Depends what business you have in mind,' he rasped, then took her roughly by the arm. 'Oh, come on, we've kept Chuck waiting long enough as it is. Just be warned that this hot-and-cold game you're playing is mighty dangerous.'

Lorinda knew what he meant. He thought she had chosen the outfit to be deliberately provocative. After her lack of response last night, he thought she was playing cat and mouse with him. He would never believe this was the first outfit that had come to her hand. Come to think of it, she was not entirely sure what demon had prompted her to choose these clothes. *Was* she playing cat and mouse with him? She hadn't been aware of it, but maybe she wasn't being completely honest even with herself as to what she wanted.

She dismissed such disturbing thoughts and concentrated on keeping up with Race's long strides as he headed towards the helipad. On board the helicopter, Chuck Rider was slumped forward in the pilot's seat with his cap pulled down over his eyes. He straightened up when he heard them approach. 'Thought you'd changed your minds, folks,' he drawled, with a grin at Lorinda.

'Sorry to have kept you waiting,' she said as he helped her into the passenger seat beside Race.

'No problem, that's what I'm here for.'

As they flew over the Great Barrier Reef towards Cairns, she marvelled again at the splendour of the island-studded sea spread out beneath them. Some of the islands were no more than tiny outcrops of coral jutting above the swirling waters. Others, like Windi Bay, were fringed with golden beaches and coconut palms and were popular tourist resorts.

'How many islands do you think there are down there?' Chuck asked her above the noise of the whirling rotors.

'A couple of hundred,' she hazarded.

'Would you believe more than six hundred?' he grinned.

Her eyes widened. 'So many! But tell me, is it true that the Reef is really a living thing?'

He nodded. '*It* is really *them*—thousands of small coral animals which have built their little limestone palaces off the coast here, to make up the reef. And even that's a misnomer. There's not just one reef, but many, interspersed with the rock and coral islands you can see below us.'

Eagerly, she drank in the magnificent changes of colour which could be clearly seen from their vantage point. The sea varied from the most delicate greens to the deepest blues where the coral banks and ramparts of the reef gave way to deep and twisting channels. Only once she looked at Race sitting beside her in the passenger seat, but he was deep in his own thoughts, ignoring both her and Chuck. She was not sure he had even heard Chuck's impromptu tour guide performance, but when Chuck tentatively suggested she might like to have dinner with him some time, Race abruptly came to life.

'Much as I admire your good taste, Rider,' he drawled, 'Lorinda is not free to accept. By the time we fly back with you, she'll be wearing my ring on her finger.'

Her cheeks burned with embarrassment. How dared he! She had a good idea what Chuck must think of her for encouraging him while her supposed fiancé was sitting beside her. It seemed it was all right for Race to turn to Simone while he was engaged to her, but she was not to be permitted the same liberty. What baffled her was why he insisted on carrying this farce to the point of actually buying her a ring. Her mother was almost well enough now to cope with the truth, and after tomorrow there would be nothing more that Simone could do to her, so they could have ended the charade without going to such lengths.

Although hampered by her safely belt, she made an elaborate show of turning away from Race, but he foiled her by sliding an arm around her shoulders and drawing her close to him. She turned herself to stone in his arms, but he did not seem to notice and her body burned where it was pressed against his. A sensation like fire tore along her veins and her pulses raced. What on earth was the matter with her? She had never been so physically affected by anyone in her life. She tried to pull away, but his hold tightened.

'You might as well relax . . . darling,' he murmured in her ear.

'What do you think you're doing?' she demanded in an undertone.

'Just making sure my bride-to-be is comfortable and safe,' he said suavely.

Lorinda wanted to scream at him to stop this, that his constant reminders of their supposed status were tearing her apart. With all her heart, she wished she could *really* be engaged to him, yet knowing him and the kind of life he led, she knew it was impossible. So why did he insist on tormenting her with something she could never have? He had said nothing about spending the night with Simone, even though she had met him coming out of the dancer's suite, so perhaps he thought she was as broadminded as they apparently were. Well, she wasn't and could never be, no matter how Race manipulated their undeniable physical attraction.

She was relieved when they finally touched down at Cairns Airport. To her surprise, they were met by a sleek grey limousine which drew up on the tarmac alongside the helicopter. A uniformed chauffeur got out and opened the rear door for them.

'You're determined to rub it in, aren't you?' she muttered at Race as he helped her down from the helicopter.

He was unperturbed. 'I don't know what you mean.'

'Yes, you do. You know I regret that we ever got into this, even if it was for my benefit.'

'I'm glad you remember that, occasionally,' he said mildly.

She felt like shaking him. 'That's no reason to turn it into a three-ring circus!'

Ignoring her protests, he steered her to the gleaming car and handed her into the back seat. It would have been quite an experience, she reflected, if she hadn't been so annoyed with Race for making such a fuss about the whole thing. She was even less pleased when the car pulled away without Chuck.

'What's he supposed to do all day?' she demanded.

'Wait for us to come back, like the well paid employee he is.'

She gave him a withering look. 'You're impossible! I believe you *like* riding roughshod over everybody. You talk about me having problems, but you've got a few of your own—one of them being your insufferable ego!' Fuming, she sank back against the luxuriously upholstered seat and waited for him to deny the accusation.

Instead, he gazed through the tinted window with every appearance of being vitally interested in the passing scene. Then he turned slowly back to her. 'I don't know what's gotten into you today, Lorinda. You're so damned defensive all of a sudden. Is it because of what nearly happened last night—or are you sore because nothing did?'

It was so close to the truth that she felt shattered. Ever since she awoke this morning, she'd been telling herself that she had done the right thing, that she was glad he had turned to Simone—but part of her was hurt to think that he could arouse her to fever pitch last night, then make love to another woman without a backward glance. She slumped in her seat.

'Hit the nail on the head, did I?'

'Leave me alone,' she said crossly, then in a bid to change the subject, 'Where are we going anyway?'

'The Parakeelya Hotel,' he told her. 'I've reserved a suite there for us.'

'A hotel? I thought we were supposed to be shopping for an engagement ring?' she said anxiously, trying to keep her voice steady.

'We are,' he agreed. That was all he would say until the limousine pulled up under the canopy of a magnificent multi-storeyed building on the waterfront facing Trinity Inlet. The management was obviously expecting Race, for a man came hurrying up to him and all but bowed as he showed them to the elevator. It sped them swiftly to the top floor of the building, where there was only one suite—the penthouse. Lorinda grew more and more agitated as the minutes passed and they were shown into an opulent suite. A bottle of champagne, its sides glistening at the change from refrigerator to ice bucket, stood ready between two silver goblets.

Lorinda waited until the manager had left, then whirled on Race. 'I take it this is your idea of a joke?'

'What do you mean by that?'

She indicated the huge living room and the bedrooms she could glimpse beyond. 'All this. It doesn't look anything like a jewellery shop to me, so I've got a pretty good idea what you've got in mind, and it isn't going to work!'

Suddenly, infuriatingly, he broke into peals of laughter. 'My heavens, woman, you think I brought you here to seduce you!'

'Well, didn't you?'

'Of course not. You made your feelings perfectly clear on that score last night—I respected that, didn't I?'

'Yes,' she admitted reluctantly. Only because he had Simone waiting in the room next door, she thought crossly, then realised she was being unfair. 'All right, I apologise for thinking . . . what I did.'

He strode over to the ice bucket and poured two glasses of the foaming liquid, passed one to her then raised his glass in a toast. 'To a total innocent!'

She took a quick sip to hide the rush of colour to her cheeks. Total innocent and complete idiot, he was probably thinking. 'Well, you have to admit it's a pretty strange way to go shopping,' she said defensively.

'I don't know how to put this without sounding immodest, but not if you're me,' he explained. 'You haven't been aware of it in Windi Bay because it's a fairly exclusive resort, but if I walked down the main street of this town I wouldn't get two blocks before I had a crowd around me demanding autographs.'

'Oh, the price of fame,' she murmured sarcastically.

'Care to try it?' he asked, and the threatening undertone in his voice told her he meant what he said.

'No, thanks, I'll take your word for it. But I don't understand how we're supposed to do our shopping from this room—by telephone?'

'More or less. The head of Du Val Diamonds should be arriving at any moment with a selection for Madam's pleasure.'

Lorinda gasped as she recognised the name of the world-famous jeweller. 'He's coming here?'

As if on cue, the telephone buzzed. Race picked up the receiver and listened, then muttered a curt 'Ask him to come up.'

The jeweller, who introduced himself as Paul du Val, was an unprepossessing little man with thinning hair and rimless glasses. He looked incredibly frail and vulnerable to be carrying around a fortune in diamonds, but as he moved, Lorinda caught the glint of metal under his arm and realised that he was carrying a gun. A security guard was stationed at the elevator and another in the hotel lobby, Mr du Val informed them as he spread out his wares on a velvet-lined tray.

Lorinda felt like Alice in Wonderland as she surveyed the exquisite gems. Tentatively, she reached out a hand to the tray, then withdrew it quickly, conscious of the enormous value the pieces probably represented.

'Please, feel free to examine any of them,' Mr du Val encouraged her. 'You will find they are all a perfect fit.'

'But how?' she asked, baffled. She glanced at Race. 'Did you . . .'

He nodded. 'I took the liberty of measuring one of your rings at the resort, then I wired du Val the size.'

It was like a dream, she thought as she tried on first one ring and then another. Of course, she could not possibly keep any of them. She would have to choose one now to satisfy Race, but it would only be on loan until they could get out of the engagement.

'They all look so lovely,' she mused. Her eye was drawn to a coral stone set in yellow gold and surrounded by diamonds, but Race gently took it from her finger and replaced it with another.

'That's more like it.'

It was beyond doubt the most beautiful jewel she had ever seen in her life, and du Val beamed when she said so. 'This design won last year's International Award for women's dress rings,' he enthused. 'The heart-cut centre diamond is naturally canary-coloured and weighs one full carat. The pear-cut shoulder diamonds weigh a further carat and the setting is eighteen-carat gold.'

'We'll take it,' Race decided.

There seemed no point in protesting that she was supposed to be the one making the choice because it was easily the loveliest piece on the tray. Besides, it would belong to Race in the end anyway, so he should have the final say. As she looked at it glinting on her finger, she was tormented by jealousy as she thought of the woman who would one day wear it as Race's real bride-to-be.

Mr du Val was delighted with Race's choice, and after the two men had settled the business details, the jeweller left with his security guards and lunch was served in their suite. It must have been ordered beforehand, because Lorinda hadn't heard Race call for room service, yet punctually at one o'clock, a waiter wheeled in an ornate silver trolley laden with pâté, lobster salads and tropical fruit cocktails in sherry. 'We can serve ourselves, thanks,' Race told the waiter, who bowed in acknowledgement and left.

While Race uncorked the wine, Lorinda sat at the intimate table set under a huge picture window and gazed out at the view of the bay which stretched to the horizon.

'Impressive, isn't it?' he asked as he slid into the seat opposite her and poured wine into her glass.

'It's so misty—like a dream,' she said. 'I wish . . .'

'What do you wish?'

'Oh, nothing important.' She had been going to say she wished things were different between them, that she was an ordinary girl who'd been brought up in an ordinary suburban family and that he was the man next door. But then, she told herself, he wouldn't be Race Wolfendale and she wouldn't be hopelessly in love with him and unable to do anything about it.

'I know what I wish,' he said, smiling into her eyes. 'I wish you'd tell me what you've got against me, Lorinda Fleming. I know you care for me—it shows, so don't deny it. So why are you so determined to shut me out of your life?'

She could have said, 'It's because you're tall, dark and a stranger who has stolen my heart just as the gypsy said you would. And that I'm scared of committing myself to you and then being left high and dry.' She could have said all that, but she was afraid he would deny it and she would have no defence left. Because she had her mother's marriage as proof of how it would be, and no amount of words could change that. So instead, she said lightly, 'You said yourself I'm looking for a father figure, not a lover.'

His fist came crashing down on the table, rattling the fragile porcelain. 'Stop it, Lorinda! Why can't you be honest with me?'

'Like you've been honest with me, I suppose?'

'What in hell's that supposed to mean?'

'I think you know,' she said quietly. 'I saw you coming out of Simone's suite this morning, remember?'

'And you think that I . . . that we . . .'

'Yes.'

'Dammit, Lorinda, you must have a pretty low opinion of me!'

Not of you, of the kind of man your profession turns you into, she thought miserably. She noticed that in his indignation, he didn't deny that he had slept with Simone. Well, it was about what she expected, so she shouldn't be surprised. 'Can we change the subject?' she asked with what dignity she could muster.

'With pleasure,' he said icily. 'Since you seem to have me tried and hanged already, there's no point in my denying it, is there?'

That was how it was for the rest of the meal, and she found no pleasure in the tender lobster with its piquant orange salad, or in the fruit cocktail which she only pushed around the goblet with a spoon. Race's anger was like a tangible presence in the room, making the sunny brightly lit suite seem dark and threatening.

She was glad when he announced that it was time to return to the airport where Chuck was waiting with the helicopter.

They hardly spoke to one another on the flight back, causing Chuck to glance at them speculatively, but he said nothing, and soon they were coming in to land at Windi Bay.

'Looks like we've got a reception committee,' the pilot observed as he set the 'copter down.

Oh lord, not another reporter wanting quotes from the 'happy couple'! Lorinda thought, feeling anything but radiant. But the man waiting at the edge of the helipad carried no camera or notepad. As they walked towards him, Lorinda thought he looked familiar. It couldn't be! But it was. The boyish good looks were still there, and the remembered thatch of straw-coloured hair falling raffishly over one eye. She hesitated for the merest fraction of a second, then hurled herself at the man and was gathered in his arms at once.

Under Race's sullen gaze, he smothered the top of her head with kisses. 'How's my little Anni-Lori?' he asked, using his pet name for her.

'It's so good to see you!' she breathed through tears of surprise and gladness. 'But where . . . how?'

'There's time enough for all that,' he said affectionately, and kept an arm around her shoulders as she turned to Chuck and Race.

'Race Wolfendale, Chuck Rider, this is . . .'

Before she could finish, the man stepped forward and thrust his hand out to Race. 'Rick Brennan—glad to meet a fellow entertainer.'

CHAPTER EIGHT

IN her own room, Lorinda whirled on Rick. 'Why didn't you tell them that you're my father?'

'Don't make a mountain out of a molehill, Anni-Lori. Does it matter who they think I am?'

Yes, it does, she thought, fighting to hold back her tears of frustration. She had seen Race's face after Rick took her in his arms. First, she caught a glimpse of little-boy hurt in his dark eyes, then his expression had turned to one of disgust which stabbed her to her very core. Then he had turned and walked away without a word. 'They think you're my boy-friend!' she said despairingly.

He put an arm around her shoulders. 'And aren't I?' he queried playfully. 'You always were my best girl, you know.'

She pulled away from him. 'That was a long time ago. It would have been nice to have an occasional reminder instead of just memories for all these years.'

'Now don't pretend you weren't glad to see me,' he said irritably. 'That reaction out at the helipad couldn't have been play-acting.'

'If I hadn't been so surprised to find you there, I might have reacted differently.'

'I don't think so. That first reaction was the genuine one. It's only now you've had time to think about it that you're wondering if it was appropriate. Your conscience is telling you that you should be disapproving, but your heart is contradicting you. Am I right?'

Reluctantly, she nodded. Her first instinct had been to run to him like the child she had been when he left, as if he had been gone for a day instead of half her lifetime. Only now, she became annoyed at herself. For her mother's sake as much as for her own, she should have been cold and unforgiving towards him to punish him for having deserted them and to show that he couldn't just walk back into her life any time he chose. But even as her brain formulated the cutting things she ought to say, she knew she couldn't do it. Whatever he was, he was still her father and she *was* glad to see him. Ever since she was a child she had dreamed that he would one day walk back into her life. Until now, it had been a kind of insurance against facing the fact that he had left her, although deep inside, she had never really believed he would return. Now, the impossible had happened and she didn't have the strength to send him away when her every instinct was to beg him to stay.

Rick watched her, his expression triumphant. 'I'm glad you feel that way. A lot of people would feel they had to punish me for leaving, but not my little Anni-Lori . . . and you're still that, no matter how grown-up and beautiful you've become since I saw you last. How long ago was it?'

'Twelve years,' she said, unable to keep the bitterness out of her voice.

He cupped her chin in one hand and tilted her face to his. 'I know it's been a long time, honey, but I have kept an eye on you and your mother from a distance. I knew you were doing all right.'

'But you never called, never wrote. Why?'

'I wanted to, believe me, but the longer I was away, the harder it was to get in touch, until I convinced myself you were better off without me. Which you were,' he said, turning away from her. 'I wasn't even making enough to keep myself, far less to support a wife and kid.'

Lorinda winced at the slang expression. Didn't he realise that the 'kid' was a thinking, feeling human being who for years believed she was somehow to blame for her father going away? As a child, she had prayed every night for God to make her a better person so that her father would want to live with her again. Only much later, as she grew to adulthood, was she able to accept that the flaw was in Rick, not in herself. And he thought they were better off without him! 'If you only knew!' she breathed.

'Knew what?'

'It doesn't matter now. But you would have been welcome to come back. We'd have managed.'

'That's all water under the bridge now,' he said a little roughly, then his tone softened. 'The point is, I'm here now—that's all that matters.'

Nothing had changed, she reflected. He was still able to sweep aside twelve years of heartbreak and think only of the present. Try as she might, she couldn't set the past aside so easily. 'You still haven't told me why you came back,' she ventured.

'I read about you getting engaged and being here on the island. I was on the mainland, not far away—I just wanted to see you again, to wish you well.'

'I see.' How she wished she could believe that was his only motive, but her doubts persisted. 'Are you planning to see Mum?'

'I don't think she would want to see me.'

'Oh, but . . .'

'Leave it!' His whiplash tone cut through her small store of courage and she backed away. Tiredly, he ran a hand through his hair which, close up, looked to her like a hairpiece and was probably just as much an illusion as the boyish looks and manner he affected. 'I'm sorry, Anni-Lori. This has been an emotional meeting for me, too, more than I expected, actually.

What existed between your mother and me was over a long time ago. I'd rather hear about you and Race—after all, your life together is just beginning.'

'No, it's not,' she said flatly.

'What's that supposed to mean?'

'The engagement was a fake, a publicity stunt,' she said, improvising. He had no need to know the whole story.

He looked angry, then suddenly his face broke into a wide grin. 'I see, a publicity stunt. You wouldn't be going to tell me you're "just good friends", now would you?'

It was the same expression her mother had used, and in show business, it meant that the love affair existed but was not for public scrutiny. 'No, it's nothing like that,' she said quickly. 'There was never anything between us—it was just a good way of drumming up some headlines.'

'Then why do you care if he thinks I'm your boy-friend?' he asked quietly.

The anguish in her expression betrayed her. There was no point in pretending that she didn't care about Race, because she wasn't a good enough actress to hide her real feelings. 'All right, so I am in love with him,' she admitted. 'But it doesn't change anything. The engagement will be called off as soon as we leave the island.'

He bit his lip thoughtfully. 'Just tell me one thing, Anni-Lori—why?'

'You mean why did we pretend to be engaged?'

'No. Why do you want me to think the engagement is a fake? Are you scared I might want something from you?'

Why wouldn't he believe her? 'No, it's nothing like that. I've told you, there was never a real engagement, whether you believe it or not.' She turned her face away from him to hide the tears that sprang unbidden to her eyes. 'Think what you like, it's the truth.'

Gently, he rested a hand on her shoulder. 'All right, honey, I won't push it. But I don't pretend to understand what's going on here. Maybe I will when I've been here a little longer.'

'You're staying on the island?'

'Here, in this room, as it happens. Gerhardt Muller didn't have a vacant room for tonight, but when I explained who I was, he suggested I use the spare bed in your suite just for one night. I'll be able to have a room of my own tomorrow.'

'But you can't stay here!' she exclaimed. 'It's bad enough everyone thinks you're my boy-friend. What will they think if you spend the night here?'

'I'll just tell them who I am.'

She could imagine the knowing looks if she suddenly announced that he was her father. No one would believe such a thing, least of all Race, especially since Rick treated her more like girl-friend than a daughter, and she was so used to thinking of him as Rick that she couldn't imagine calling him Dad, even if he would permit it.

'Don't look so scandalised,' he said. 'Even if I grant that you and Race are not really engaged, I don't believe a red-blooded daughter of mine has been on an island for a week with a man like him and nothing's happened, so it's not as if your reputation was at stake.'

'Whatever the reality, I *am* supposed to be engaged,' she reminded him. 'What will everyone think if I share my room with another man?'

'If by everyone, you mean Race Wolfendale, it shouldn't matter if the engagement is as phoney as you tell me.' He studied her closely. 'Unless . . . you really care about what he thinks.'

'I've already told you I'm in love with him. That doesn't mean it works both ways,' she flung at him.

'Then maybe my arrival is just what's needed to persuade him,' Rick suggested.

'I don't see what good that would do.'

'A bit of uncertainty is good for a relationship. It adds spice to a marriage—it did for your mother and me, didn't it?'

'No, it didn't,' she denied bitterly. 'Or weren't you aware that while she was pretending not to care, she was breaking her heart?'

'Oh, come on now, Anni, you were too young to know about such things,' he assured her, but some of the conviction had gone out of his voice. 'Your mother and I had an understanding. These days, they even have a name for it—open marriage.'

'You may have felt that way, but I'm sure Mum didn't,' she told him. 'You forget, she and I have spent a long time together. I probably know her better than you ever did. Do you know, since you left she's never even looked at another man.'

Rick stared at her as if she had struck him with a heavy object. 'Well, I'll be damned! She let me think . . .' His voice broke. 'Did I really make her so unhappy?' She nodded, and his face contorted with the shock of the discovery. 'My word, Anni, all these years I never knew—I swear it!'

'Would it have changed anything if you had?' she asked, surprising herself.

'Yes, I think it would,' he said slowly. 'Because she never said anything, and I was pretty certain she knew I was playing around . . . I thought . . . I thought she didn't care.' All at once, he buried his head in his hands, and to her horror she saw that his shoulders were shaking.

She had never felt so helpless in her life. 'Don't

torture yourself,' she pleaded. 'You said yourself it's all water under the bridge.' Suddenly she remembered the time. 'I'd better get ready for dinner. Race will be expecting me.' At least, she hoped he was still talking to her after the scene at the helipad this afternoon. She looked down at her left hand where the huge diamond shone mockingly up at her. It seemed an eternity since this morning, when Race had placed it on her finger. Wearily she made herself get up and go to the wardrobe to select a gown for the evening, and took it into the bathroom to change.

By the time she emerged, dressed and with her hair brushed back and held in place by two tortoiseshell combs, Rick had pulled himself together. 'Are you coming down to the restaurant?'

'You go along. I'll come down shortly.'

Lorinda picked up her purse and walked out of the suite, leaving him still sitting on the edge of the bed staring into space.

What a mess it all was, she thought as she made her way slowly towards the Neptune Room. All those years wasted because Rick believed that Arna didn't care about him, while she had only been trying to give him the freedom she thought would make him happy. She was right to avoid such entanglements, she told herself, because they only led to heartache and misery.

Silently, she blessed the gypsy for her timely warning. She had still fallen in love with the tall dark stranger, but at least she was aware of the risks in letting him know how she felt. Because if he knew she loved him, he would promise her the earth just as Rick had done when he proposed to Arna, and she was sure Race wouldn't be able to keep his promises any more than Rick could. Her father might well be sorry now for the way he had acted, but it was too late. Too many people had been hurt, herself among them. Her life wasn't going to be a repeat of her mother's, she vowed, even if it meant she had to spend the rest of her days alone.

In the lobby, she bumped into Gerhardt—literally. 'Steady there!' he cautioned goodnaturedly.

'I was dreaming and not looking where I was going.' On impulse she took the magnificent ring from her finger and held it out to him. 'Could you put this in the hotel safe for me, Gerhardt?'

He whistled appreciatively as he hefted it in his palm. 'I certainly will. But I wonder how you can bear to take it from your finger, given what it symbolises.'

This was a line of discussion Lorinda was determined not to pursue. Her emotions had been through the mangle enough for one day. 'It's just that it's so valuable. I would hate to lose it on the beach or in the sea.'

'Of course, I understand,' he assured her. But his eyes were soft with concern as he watched her walk into the Neptune room.

Race was alone at a table set for two. To her relief there was no sign of Simone for the moment. Race stood up as she approached and his glance flickered over her left hand. He must have noticed that she had removed his ring, but he said nothing about it. 'I'm surprised you honoured me with your presence tonight,' he jibed instead.

Lorinda took the chair he held out for her and fixed her eyes on the tablecloth to avoid meeting his mocking gaze. 'Don't, Race,' she begged. 'It's not what you think.'

'Oh no . . . *Anni-Lori?*' he sneered.

She flinched at the derision in his voice. 'I'll explain later, but not now. I'd like a drink.'

He raised a curious eyebrow at this, but ordered the gin and tonic she requested. She sipped it thankfully, feeling the liquid sting her throat and bring colour flooding back to her cheeks. Gradually her nerves steadied sufficiently so she could make polite conversation with him, telling him about Max's call earlier and the good publicity the opening had received.

'That's all terrific, I'm sure,' he said dryly. 'But I can talk business with my manager. With you, I'd like to discuss more personal matters—us, for instance. Or is that all off now the boy-friend's in the picture?'

'It isn't off, because it was never on,' she said wearily. With a feeling of desolation, she knew she wasn't going to tell him who Rick was after all. As long as Race thought he was an old flame rekindled, he would leave her alone and she would be in less danger of giving away her real feelings.

'For heaven's sake, Lorinda, he's old enough to be your father!' Then he looked at her in sudden understanding. 'That's it, isn't it? Of course—he fits the image perfectly, probably wrapping you in a cocoon of paternal love and security. I'd forgotten it's the only kind of relationship that interests you.'

His comment struck her like a physical blow, but if he thought he could reach her by hurting her, he was wrong. She schooled her features into an expressionless mask. 'Rick and I . . . understand each other,' she said carefully.

'That's obvious,' he retorted. 'It's also obvious that you're so undemanding sexually that he feels free to flirt with any female in the room.'

She followed his glance to the bar where she saw Rick had settled on a stool beside a long-legged showgirl. Their heads were close together and it seemed he had forgotten her existence for the present.

'How come he only showed up now?' Race was asking.

'We ... split up ... a long time ago.'

'And he heard about your engagement to me, is that it?' She nodded miserably. 'Well, from the way he's acting with Doreen over there, I guess it wasn't jealousy that brought him to the island.'

'No, it wasn't. I really don't know why he came, but he'll tell me in his own good time.'

'No need to wait. I can enlighten you here and now. He said he's an entertainer. I'll bet as soon as lover-boy found out you were engaged to me, he thought he'd get you to use your influence to help his career along.'

'No!' The cry was out before she could bite it back, but it was half in protest and half in fear that he might be right. Why hadn't she thought of that herself? It was quite in character for Rick Brennan to try to use her as he'd always used everyone.

Race watched the tragic play of emotions across her features and his expression softened. Gently he placed a hand on hers. 'I'm sorry, Lorinda. You obviously thought he came back because he loved you, but it doesn't look that way from where I sit. Why don't you ask him—maybe I've got it all wrong?'

But seeing Rick perched at the bar with his arm around the showgirl, Lorinda had the sinking sensation that Race was right. It was the only sensible explanation. She could have worked it out for herself. But she had believed what she wanted to believe, that Rick had come back because he loved his daughter and wanted to see her again, just as he said. For a short time, she'd known what it was to have a father again, even if he didn't act much like one. Now Race had removed her rose-coloured glasses, and her eyes began to brim with tears.

Quickly she pushed her chair away from the table and stood up. 'I'm not feeling very well, Race, you'll have to excuse me.'

He reached for her hand. 'Lorinda, we've got to talk. In a few minutes I've promised an interview to a national magazine. They flew a photo-journalist up from Sydney or I'd gladly call it off. But after I've done the late show, I'll call by your room.'

'There's no need, I'm all right—really,' she assured him, mustering a smile. Then she fled from the room before the brittle mask shattered completely.

By the time she reached the sanctuary of her suite the tears were running in rivers down her cheeks and her mascara was smudged into black streaks. The face which stared back at her from the mirror looked like a brokenhearted clown.

She must have cried herself to the point of exhaustion, because the next thing she knew was the scratching of a key in the lock. Disorientated, she sat up on the bed, aware that she still wore her strapless evening gown which was now tear-stained and crumpled where she had lain on it.

The door opened to admit Rick, who had obviously enjoyed quite a few more drinks at the bar after she left. Lorinda glanced at her watch, but it had stopped. 'What time is it?'

'After midnight. Anything wrong with that?' His face was flushed, but his speech was surprisingly clear. He hardly glanced at her and seemed unaware of her dishevelled appearance.

'No, there's nothing wrong in that,' she murmured, but was talking to his back as he disappeared into the bathroom. She heard the shower running, and soon after, he began to sing disjointed snatches of song. His voice was still good, she thought distractedly. If he'd had the discipline to work at his craft he might have been a successful singer, perhaps as successful as Race Wolfendale.

Thinking of Race reminded her of his suspicions at

dinner and she resolved to ask Rick about it when he emerged from the shower. While she waited for him, she took the chance to slip out of the crumpled gown and into a nightdress, the first one she had worn since coming to the island. Rick was to have the divan bed near the balcony so she turned it down ready for him then found pyjamas and dressing gown in his battered suitcase and passed them to him around the bathroom door.

By the time he came out, she was sitting up in bed with her arms clasped around her knees.

The shower seemed to have refreshed him and he looked enquiringly at her. 'Still wide awake?'

'I couldn't go to sleep. Not until I'd had a chance to ask you something.'

'Oh, and what might that be, Anni-Lori?'

Her throat tightened at the sound of the pet name. 'Please don't call me that,' she said huskily.

He frowned. 'It was good enough for you when you were a little girl.'

'But I'm not a little girl any more. I'm a grown woman and you can't charm me quite as easily as you could then.'

'You sound just like your mother,' he said softly. Had she imagined it, or was there the merest trace of regret in his tone?

'If I do, I'm proud of it,' she said, lifting her head. 'She did a fine job of bringing me up, even though it was far from easy for her.'

'No need to keep reminding me,' he said gruffly, 'I've said it to myself a million times since I've been on my own.' He brushed a hand across his eyes as if to brush away the troublesome memories. 'Now what was it you waited up half the night to ask me?'

'Why did you really come here?' There, it was said. She found she was holding her breath as she hoped beyond hope that he would give the answer she longed to hear.

'I've told you—it's been so long. When I found you were here through the newspaper stories . . .'

Instinctively she knew he was lying. 'No, I want the real reason,' she insisted.

He stared at her for a moment which stretched into infinity. Then he expelled a heavy breath. 'Do you want to know why I came?' he demanded harshly. His tone frightened her, but she nodded. 'All right, since you asked, I came to blackmail you into getting me a contract here.'

So Race had been right all along, as he had been right about so many things since they met. Her face paled and the room tilted crazily until she was afraid she was going to faint. 'Blackmail me? What are you talking about, Rick?'

When she swayed, he moved towards her automatically and now he sat down on the edge of the bed and drew her to him. She was repelled by the smell of whisky on his breath, but she had no strength left to resist, so she lay against his chest like a rag doll, feeling the coarse linen of his dressing gown rub against her cheek.

'There, there,' he said gently. 'I didn't mean to frighten you like that, but you asked for the truth. And you said yourself, you're a grown woman now.'

'Please go on,' she whispered.

He held her against him and spoke into her hair so his voice was muffled. 'After I left you and your mother, everything was great at first. But I missed you two more than I believed possible and I started to drink heavily. I missed a few performances, got fired, and that just made me drink more until I was drinking more hours than I was working. But I woke up in time, I swear. Only by then there wasn't a producer or club manager who'd hire me. When I read about you getting engaged to a big star like Race Wolfendale, it was like the answer to a prayer. I thought you'd be able to pull a few strings, help me get my career going again.'

Lorinda looked up at him in confusion. 'But asking for my help isn't blackmail, surely?'

He pressed her against his shoulder again. 'Don't look at me with those big sad eyes! You make me feel like more of a scoundrel than I do already. The papers also said something else—that Arna was recovering from a heart attack.'

Her eyes widened. 'You knew about that? I didn't know how to tell you—you always hated illness so.'

'I still do. But when I found out she had a bad heart, I knew you wouldn't want me bothering her. And since I wasn't at all sure you'd be willing to help me after the way I'd treated you, I . . . planned to use Arna's illness to persuade you to co-operate.'

This time she pulled away in horror. 'That's despicable!' she breathed. 'To think you'd even threaten a sick woman . . . your own wife . . . to get your own way!'

'Lorinda, don't, please,' he pleaded, and there was no mistaking the pain in his voice. 'Since this afternoon, I've said all that to myself and worse.'

'Which doesn't excuse you one little bit,' she said coldly. 'When were you planning to spring your little surprise?'

He flinched at the venom in her tone. 'That's just it, I wasn't.'

'But you just said . . .'

'I know, and I intended to go through with it. But when I saw you again and discovered what a beautiful, sensitive creature my little girl had grown into, I found that you meant much more to me than I ever suspected. Then when you told me how Arna really felt about me and how she's been faithful all these years ... I couldn't go through with it. I knew I couldn't do anything to hurt you more than I've already done.'

You've done it by coming here, she thought despairingly. But he couldn't know that, and she believed him when he said he hadn't meant to hurt her further. She was astonished to find she believed everything he said. There was something pathetically convincing in the way he looked at her, his eyes begging for her understanding.

Rick held out his arms to her, and after the merest hesitation she went into them. He traced the line of a tear down her cheek. 'What's this for, Anni?'

'I'm so h-happy, Rick,' she gulped. 'You don't know how much I've missed you and wondered what you were doing.'

'About as much as I've missed you and wondered the same thing,' he said seriously. 'Look, I know I've left it a bit late and I don't know if I can change after all this time but ...'

'But what?' she prompted.

'Do you think Arna would give me another chance?'

'Only she can answer that,' she said, but the surge of gladness coursing through her told her if her mother reacted the same way, he stood a very good chance indeed.

'There's just one other thing ...'

'And what's that, Rick?'

'Do you ... could you possibly call me Dad?'

The tears started anew as she hugged him. 'I could try ... Dad.' The word sounded foreign to her ears, but it had such a warm ring to it that she knew she had been waiting for half a lifetime for the chance to say it. With the last barrier down, they began to exchange news and nostalgic memories from her childhood.

They were sitting propped up against Lorinda's pillows, exchanging laughing reminiscences, when the door opened. Rick must have forgotten to lock it when he came in, she thought, then blanched as she saw who was standing in the doorway.

'Race!' she said uncertainly, frightened by the thunderous expression on his face.

'Yes, it's me. Evidently you forgot that I was to drop by for a chat after the late show. It seems you had other things on your mind.'

'Race, wait!'

But he had gone, slamming the door so violently that it rattled on its hinges. She sagged back against the pillow like a pricked balloon.

Rick watched her worriedly. 'You really do love him, don't you?' When she didn't respond, he went on. 'Poor kid! It was bad enough that your mother had the rotten luck to fall for an entertainer, without making the same mistake.'

'You can't help whom you love,' she whispered. But you *can* control what you do about it, she reminded herself. Race now believed that she and Rick were lovers instead of father and daughter and the discovery had driven him away more surely than anything she could have said to him. The thought that she had achieved what she set out to do gave her no comfort, only an aching sense of loss. It would pass, she told herself; it had to. At least by sending him away now, she was safe from a lifetime of torment, never knowing when he would decide to end the relationship. By then, the pain would be too much to hear.

It was almost more than she could bear now, she thought a little later as she curled up in her own bed and reached for the light switch. From the sound of his slow, even breathing, Rick was already asleep. He had said what he could to comfort her and when she didn't respond, he had suggested they get some rest. They would both feel better in the morning, he assured her.

Taking stock of her shattered emotions as she lay in the darkened room, she doubted it. At least she knew Race would not be disturbed by her rejection for long. He would probably seek solace in Simone's arms as he had done before when Lorinda wouldn't sleep with him. She was tortured by visions of him in Simone's bed, his dark head next to hers on the pillows. This must have been how mother felt every time she knew Rick was with another woman, she thought, and her heart went out to sweet, generous Arna. If the pain of loving someone like Race was as bad as this now, what must it have been like for Arna after years of marriage to Rick? No wonder she had never risked marrying again.

Lorinda hardly dared hope that her mother would give Rick another chance after so long, but she drew a little comfort from the knowledge that Rick was prepared to try. Hugging her pillow which was damp from her tears, she clung to that thought, anything to stop herself from thinking about the look in Race's eyes when he found her there with Rick. But try as she might to dismiss it from her mind, she was haunted by the memory of his expression. She had seen no trace of accusation in it, although he was entitled to that, given that she was supposedly engaged to him. Rather, his eyes had been dark with shock and hurt ... and something else she didn't understand. Surely it couldn't have been jealousy? That would mean ... no, she mustn't even consider such a thing, now or ever again.

'Be kind to him, Simone,' she whispered into the darkness just before she fell into a troubled sleep.

CHAPTER NINE

BY next morning she knew there was only one thing she could do, and that was to leave the island as soon as possible. If she could only get away from Race's disturbing presence she would have a chance to get over him and start again. Still, it would take a long time before she was truly free of his memory, she feared. If she ever was, a traitorous voice inside argued.

Fortunately, now that Rick had decided to see Arna again, he was only too eager to leave for Sydney, and he agreed at once to Lorinda's suggestion that they fly out this afternoon instead of waiting until the next morning.

'There's only one thing,' he began awkwardly.

'And what's that?'

'I don't have a cent to my name. I used my last cash reserve to fly out here to see you.'

Lorinda laughed aloud with relief. 'If that's all, I can pay for your ticket to Sydney.' She went on to tell him about the money her old nurse, Janet Ryland, had bequeathed to her in her will.

He whistled softly. 'Who'd have guessed old Janey had a bean!' Then he flushed as he saw his daughter's face darken. 'I didn't mean to sound callous,' he said quickly. 'I was very fond of Janey, too, in my own way. Hell, Lorinda, don't look like that. I told you I can't change my spots overnight.'

She squeezed his hand. 'It's all right. It's just that I kept in touch with Janey from the time she stopped working for you, so her death hit me pretty hard. I hadn't realised how much she meant to me.'

He smiled at her. 'Just the way I felt about you, Anni-Lori. It's kind of a blow to your independence when you find out what a hold another person can have over your emotions.'

She said nothing, but she knew exactly what he meant. Since she was a child she had been careful never to let anyone come close enough to hurt her. When she received word that Janey was dead the shock forced her to face the fact that she *did* love the old nurse, no matter what other name she tried to give the relationship. Now she had to accept that Race had also staked a claim to her heart, in spite of all her efforts to resist. She had been so sure that the wall she had built around her emotions was enough to protect her, but now she wondered whether any defence would be proof against a man like Race Wolfendale.

'That was a big sigh, honey. Sorry to be leaving the island?'

'Not really,' she responded. 'It's a beautiful place, but I'll be glad to get home again.'

'The old saw about parting being such sweet sorrow, huh?' he teased. 'You want to go, but part of you wants to stay.'

He couldn't know it, but that was exactly the way she felt, but not because she was leaving the island. Her feelings went much deeper than that. She was torn between wanting to run as far away from Race's arms as she possibly could and wishing she could stay with him for whatever brief time he allowed her before his fickle heart took him away. But she was reckoning without Simone, she acknowledged. He had made love to her here in this very room, knowing the dancer was waiting for him nearby. She couldn't compete with Simone, she knew. Once, Race had loved her enough to marry her, and it seemed more than a trace of that feeling still existed even though the marriage had been inexplicably brief.

'Are you packing that suitcase or dreaming into it?'

She came out of her reverie with a jolt. 'What? Oh yes, I was just thinking . . .'

'About Race Wolfendale?' Rick probed gently.

'No, of course not!' But the denial sounded hollow even to her own ears. As she folded her clothes into the case she couldn't help thinking of how Race had chosen them for her before they left Sydney. She choked back a sob as she remembered the sight of his strong, muscular hands clasping her delicate under-things as he arbitrarily chose her travel wardrobe for her. Angrily she dashed the tears away with the back of her hand and snapped the case shut, as if closing a lid on her disquieting thoughts. 'I'm ready,' she said with an assurance she did not feel.

After a final look around the suite to make sure she had forgotten nothing, she pulled the door closed for the last time and followed Rick along the covered walkway towards the main hotel building.

The lobby with its cathedral-like ceiling felt blissfully cool after the oppressive heat outside. Rick set their cases down on the gleaming tiled floor and looked around for Gerhardt. The manager was in his office, bent over some paperwork. He came out to greet them as they approached the desk.

When he saw their luggage, he frowned. 'You are leaving us already? But your booking is confirmed until tomorrow morning. There is nothing wrong, I trust?'

'No, nothing wrong, Gerhardt,' she reassured him. 'But there's nothing more I can do here, so I thought I'd take the chance to fly back to Sydney with Rick—with my father.'

Gerhardt looked over her shoulders towards the

open doors leading to the Neptune Room. 'What about tonight's show? I thought you would stay at least for the final performance.'

'All the details of the show are taken care of, so it should go off like clockwork. You don't need me in the audience, I'm sure.'

'Oh, but I do, Lorinda. I wish your stay here could have been much longer so we could get to know one another better.'

She smiled warmly at him. 'You've been very sweet to me, Gerhardt. I shan't forget it. But . . .'

He looked meaningfully towards the Neptune Room. 'I know. A simple hotel manager could not compete with the dazzling talents and personality of Race Wolfendale.' She was about to protest when he patted her hand. 'Don't say anything, little one. It has been my pleasure to look after you here. When you are Mrs Wolfendale, perhaps you will remember Windi Bay and come back here some time with your famous husband. Which reminds me, you must not leave without your magnificent engagement ring.' He turned towards his office where the safe was located, but halted when she gave a strangled cry of protest.

'No, leave it in the safe, Gerhardt! Give it to . . . to Race when he leaves, will you?'

He turned back, puzzled. 'I don't understand.'

'Race and I . . . we've . . . changed our minds,' she explained in a low voice.

'I see. I am very sorry to hear that for your sake. For my own, it gives me new hope. Perhaps you will return to Windi Bay after all.'

'Perhaps,' she agreed. But she knew in her heart that she would not return. Once she was back in Sydney it would be hard enough to forget what she had given up here on the island, without returning physically—she would do that often enough in memory, she was sure.

With a heavy heart, she thanked Gerhardt for his kindness and turned to leave. Ahead of her, through the open doors of the Neptune Room, she saw that Race and Simone were rehearsing for tonight's closing show. On the stage stood the huge wicker basket which held Simone's carpet snake, the one she used in her exotic dance, and Lorinda shuddered as she remembered the feel of the creature crawling along her body. One of the gardeners must have returned it to Simone, although she still hadn't told Lorinda how it came to be in her room. Since that night, Simone had acted as if Lorinda didn't exist, never acknowledging her presence with a word.

When they had met on the beach this morning, Simone had looked straight through her. Lorinda was relieved to note that the dancer was no longer limping as she had been earlier. Then, she had worn a look of pain, but it had been quickly masked by icy disdain, as soon as Lorinda emerged on to her balcony. When she walked on there was no trace of a limp, although Lorinda was sure she had seen it, just as she knew she had not imagined Simone's suffering look. It was the second time she had seen her like that and she couldn't help wondering what was wrong—not that she harboured any great concern for Simone after the way she had treated her. It was just that she hated to see any fellow human being suffering as Simone obviously was. Still, Simone had made it plain by her actions that she didn't want any attention paid to her problem, whatever it was, so Lorinda kept her sympathy to herself.

The sight of Race standing next to Simone, with his dark head bent close to hers over some sheet music, brought a lump to Lorinda's throat. 'Goodbye, Race darling . . .' she said to herself, and fled from the lobby.

Rick was nowhere in sight and she guessed he had gone ahead to take their luggage to the helicopter. He had refused Gerhardt's offer to call a staff member to do it, insisting that he preferred to look after himself. As she headed along the thatched-roof walkway, she heard footsteps behind her.

'Lorinda, wait!'

She looked back to see Race striding after her.

'Yes, what is it?' she asked, keeping her tone purposely cool.

'Gerhardt tells me you're leaving. Don't I even rate a goodbye?'

'Goodbye, Race,' she said calmly.

The light faded from his eyes and his expression hardened. 'I thought last night I might have been mistaken, but I wasn't, was I? It's Rick you're leaving with, isn't it?' When she nodded dumbly, he growled in frustration. 'Dammit, Lorinda, how can you *do* this? You know you care for me, yet you can just walk away like this. Is he the father figure you've been looking for—is that it?'

'You could say that.'

He took a step towards her and she wondered if he was going to hit her, so angry did he look. But instead he took both her shoulders in a fierce grip and gave her a little impatient shake.

'You're hurting me,' she whimpered, feeling the warmth of his hands through the thin fabric of her dress.

Without warning he bent his head and imprisoned her lips under his in a quick, violent kiss that set the blood pounding in her veins and left her swaying when he released her.

'Can Rick do that for you?' he demanded savagely. 'Lorinda, I want . . .' But she never found out what he wanted, because just at that moment there was a cry of alarm from the hotel lobby. They turned as one to see Gerhardt standing in the doorway.

'It's Simone—she's collapsed!' he told them, and disappeared inside again.

At once Race left her on the path and hurried back towards the hotel. Her lips still burned with the intensity of his kiss and she wanted nothing more than to run to Rick on board the helicopter and beg him to take her away from the island forever. Instead, she followed slowly after Race. Whatever she might think of Simone, it was her job to look after the dancer's wellbeing.

By the time she reached the Neptune Room, Simone was sitting on the edge of the stage, massaging her ankle with one hand. Race crouched alongside her and Lorinda felt a quick stab of pain as she looked at them together. Ashamed of such thoughts, she dismissed her own feelings and bent over Simone. 'Is there anything I can do?'

At once Simone jerked her head up and looked at Lorinda in alarm. 'I thought you'd gone,' she said coldly, and the fear Lorinda had seen in her eyes moments before was replaced by the implacable mask of hatred she was coming to expect from Simone.

'I *was* leaving,' she explained. 'When Gerhardt said you'd collapsed . . .'

'I did not collapse, I merely twisted an ankle, that's all. Gerhardt, why did you tell them I'd collapsed?'

The manager looked flustered. 'When I saw you lying there, I assumed . . .'

'Then don't!' she retorted. 'It was a foolish accident. All I need is rest and to bathe my ankle in cold water.' She smiled prettily and everyone but Lorinda relaxed visibly.

'I don't understand,' she ventured. 'This morning, I saw . . .'

The dancer fixed her with a penetrating glare. 'Yes? And what do you *think* you saw?'

Lorinda was baffled and worried. She *had* seen Simone limping in pain this morning, but just as obviously, she didn't want it mentioned now. From the way she had phrased her question, Lorinda knew she would deny it, perhaps accuse Lorinda of imagining things. Still, she was sure the two incidents were connected. But how? She would have to ask Simone as soon as possible. But when she stretched out a hand to help her up, her hand was angrily knocked aside.

'I can manage,' Simone snapped. 'I told you it was nothing. Race will give me all the help I need, won't you darling?' For answer, he helped her to her feet and she leaned gracefully against his shoulder, then turned back to Lorinda. 'Don't let me keep you. I'm sure your friend Rick must be getting impatient.'

At the mention of Rick's name, Lorinda saw Race's mouth harden into a grim line. 'You heard the lady,' he grated. 'There's no need for you to delay your flight. I can take care of Simone.'

The dancer's expression of triumph was more than she could bear, so she nodded dumbly and fled back down the path, not stopping this time until she reached the helipad where Rick was chatting to Chuck Rider. They were concerned when she told them what had delayed her, but looked relieved when she explained that Simone had done nothing worse than twist her ankle.

Still, on the flight to the mainland, she couldn't help wondering why Simone had been so frightened at seeing her again. For it *was* fear she had seen in the dancer's eyes, of that she was sure. Was she concerned that Lorinda would mention the incident on the beach this morning? And why should that frighten her?

Impatiently, she dismissed the question, since she had no answer for it, and turned her attention to the breathtaking sight of the Great Barrier Reef spread out beneath them. Gradually, Windi Bay became a palm-studded speck on the horizon until it was indistinguishable from the hundreds of other small islands dotting the azure sea below.

A lump rose to her throat as she thought of all that she was leaving behind in these islands, and she turned her head away so the others wouldn't see the errant tears which squeezed their way beneath her tightly closed lashes. It had been her choice to leave, she reminded herself, so she should not be surprised if Race turned to Simone for consolation. Perhaps they would remarry, she thought bleakly, and had a disturbing vision of Race slipping the magnificent engagement ring on to Simone's finger. She hoped he would be happy with her. At least they shared the same profession, so Simone would not expect him to be faithful to her, especially since they had married and separated once before.

She sighed deeply. If only she could accept him on those terms, it would be so simple. But she knew she couldn't. If she ever married—and that possibility seemed as far away as Windi Bay now was—she would want it to be forever. And she had ample evidence to know that no relationship lasted forever.

The flight from Cairns to Sydney seemed interminable and, like her mood, Sydney was bleak and wet when they landed at Kingsford Smith Airport. The flight had been fully booked, but she had been able to obtain a late cancellation, so she and Rick travelled on the same flight, although in widely separated parts of the aircraft. He caught her up in the airport lounge, and as they handed in their luggage claim checks, she was surprised to see that his hands were shaking.

'Are you feeling all right?'

He laughed hollowly. 'I've got a bad case of nerves, Anni-Lori, that's all. Nothing that a double Scotch wouldn't fix.' She shot him a look of alarm and he squeezed her hand. 'Relax! That was in the bad old days. These days, I'm not as much of a drunk as some thinkle peep.'

Despite her own inner turmoil, she was forced to laugh. 'You're impossible, but I love you!'

'Let's hope your mother feels the same way! Because right now, I feel like a teenager on his first date.'

'You should have let me phone her ahead. She may not appreciate surprises in her state of health.'

'You mean her heart? But when you rang her doctor, didn't he say the best thing she could do was start living a normal life again?'

Lorinda saw her suitcase approaching on the roundabout and reached for it. Rick's case was next to hers. 'The doctor did say that,' she admitted, 'I hope he's right, that's all.'

By the time they located a taxi and endured a tense drive home through the wet, slippery streets, her nerves were stretched to breaking point and she wished more than ever that she had ignored her father's wishes and telephoned her mother ahead to break the news of Rick's return.

At least she was able to persuade Rick to wait in the coffee shop downstairs while she prepared the way for him with Arna.

As soon as she unlocked the door her nostrils were assailed with the tantalising aroma of scones baking. Even if the doctor at the convalescent home hadn't broken the news to her by phone this morning, she would have known her mother was home. She frowned, noting that every inch of the small flat gleamed, but she was not surprised. Taking things easy was not in her mother's vocabulary.

'Mum, I'm home!' she called.

At once, Arna emerged from the kitchen, wiping floury hands on her apron. 'Lorinda! I didn't expect you back until tomorrow. Is everything all right, darling?'

They flew into each other's arms and Lorinda assured her that nothing was wrong. 'My work was finished, so I was able to fly back earlier than planned, that's all. I telephoned Max from the airport to tell him.' She had also told him about Rick's return and Simone's mishap this morning. His initial alarm subsided quickly when he was told how lightly Simone had dismissed the incident.

Arna looked over Lorinda's shoulder towards the front door. 'Isn't Race with you?'

'No, he has one more show to do tonight,' she explained, then took a deep breath. The doctor had assured her that her mother was well enough to resume a normal life, in fact he said the sooner she did the better. 'You'd better sit down. I have something to tell you.'

Arna did as she was told. 'Something's happened between you and Race,' she guessed.

Lorinda took her mother's hands in her own. 'Race and I thought it over and decided we'd been a bit hasty,' she said gently. 'We're not getting married after all.'

'But if all you need is time . . .'

'That wouldn't make any difference. We . . . we decided it was better to make it a clean break.'

Her mother's eyes were dark with concern. 'I'm sorry, darling. I was so sure you were doing the right thing.'

Lorinda shrugged. 'Yes, well . . . sometimes it works

out that way. Don't worry, I'll probably fall in and out of love a dozen times before I'm ready to get married.' But even as she said it, she knew it would never happen. And she could tell from Arna's dubious frown that she knew it, too. Then she remembered Rick, waiting tensely downstairs, probably drinking his third cup of coffee by now. 'There's something else . . .' she began, watching her mother carefully. 'I flew back with someone who wants to see you, that is if you're up to it.'

'The doctor said I'm fine,' Arna insisted. 'What's all the mystery about?'

'Mum, it's Rick . . . Dad . . . we met at Windi Bay and he came back to Sydney with me.'

Arna's face paled and she gripped the edge of the couch with such force, her knuckles whitened. 'Rick's here—in Sydney?'

'Downstairs in the coffee shop, as a matter of fact. He wasn't sure you would want to see him.'

Arna pressed a hand to her mouth. 'Wasn't sure I'd want to? Heavens, how I've prayed for this moment for twelve years!'

Lorinda was baffled. She had expected almost any reaction but this one. 'You mean you still love him?'

'Still Lorinda, I don't think I ever stopped loving him!'

As she saw the joy lighting up her mother's face, Lorinda was confused. 'I don't understand, Mum. How can you feel like that after the way he's treated you?'

Her mother laughed, a silvery, carefree sound she hadn't heard since she was a child. 'Oh, my darling, love isn't conditional, like a business contract. When you love someone, it's in spite of any flaws they have. If I'd wanted a perfect husband. I would never have married your father—but I loved him, weak and all as

he was, and I never regretted a day of the time Rick
and I spent together.' Her eyes closed and her voice
thickened with nostalgia. 'We had some wonderful
times together—why do you think I've never looked at
another man after Rick?'

'I thought it was because you were soured on the
idea of marriage.'

'Just because it didn't last forever? Oh no, Lori. I
knew the risks when I agreed to marry him. But I
decided that a day of the kind of happiness I knew
when I was with Rick was worth a lifetime of
lukewarm marriage to anyone else. But what are we
sitting here for? Where is he? I'll go down and tell him
to come up!' Suddenly she jumped to her feet in panic.
'Oh dear, I look such a sight!' She cast an appealing
look at Lorinda. 'Darling, would you go down and
fetch him while I do something about my face and
hair.'

With that, she disappeared into her bedroom and
Lorinda heard her hastily rummaging through her
wardrobe. Dazed, she made her slow way downstairs.
How could she have been so wrong about her mother's
feelings? All these years, she had believed Arna had
avoided remarrying because of her experience with
Rick. Instead, it was because she loved him so much
that no other man was a match for him. It was as if a
lifetime of preconceptions had been swept away all at
once, and Lorinda felt suddenly naked and vulnerable.

Rick's face glowed when she told him of her
mother's reaction. He took the stairs two at a time, but
paused outside the door of the flat and looked at her
uncertainly.

'Go on in, it's all right,' Lorinda encouraged him.

'Do I look O.K.?'

'You look terrific. Now don't keep her waiting any
longer.'

He smiled ruefully. 'I guess twelve years is quite long enough, come to think of it.' Slowly he pushed open the door and walked into the flat.

'Hello, Rick.'

'Hello, Arna.'

Wearing her new burgundy velour house gown and with her hair freshly brushed, Arna sat on the couch looking remarkably calm. Only the way she continually twisted her handkerchief into a rope between long graceful fingers gave her away. Rick's gaze shifted from Arna's face to the handkerchief. 'This isn't easy for you either, is it?' he said softly.

Arna looked down at the crumpled handkerchief and smiled. 'I guess I'm not much of an actress, am I? Oh, Rick, I'm so glad to see you!'

Suddenly they were in each other's arms, laughing and crying at the same time. Then Rick drew Lorinda into the loving circle and they clung together. Lorinda thought she had never felt so overjoyed in her life as she was at that moment.

Later, Rick poured brandy for them all, and as they sipped it, he and Arna sat close together on the couch with their knees touching, as if they were afraid to put even the length of the room between them again. Lorinda curled up in a chair opposite them and basked in the glow of their happiness. Only for a moment, the thought of Race intruded and she pictured herself sitting in the circle of his arm, as content as Arna now looked. Quickly she thrust the thought away before it could spoil the magic of this moment.

'No one's asked yet why I left,' Rick said at last.

Lorinda tensed. It was the one question she had avoided asking him because she dreaded what the answer might be. Now it had been asked and she was hurtled back to her childhood, to the long lonely nights when she lay curled up in bed, tormenting herself with the same question, sure that she alone had been the cause of her parents' separation. They loved each other, she was sure of that, so it had to be her fault. Somehow she had done something so bad that her father couldn't stand to live in the same house with her any longer.

As an adult, she was mature enough to realise that she wasn't to blame. Two people could love each other but still be unable to live together in marriage, yet the child within her refused to accept this, even now. As she waited for Rick's explanation, her hand shook so much she had to set the brandy glass down on the coffee table to avoid spilling the contents.

To her surprise, it was Arna who spoke. 'You had a lot of growing up to do, Rick,' she said gently. 'We both did.'

He looked at her in surprise. 'You felt that way, too?'

She smiled. 'Maybe I'm a better actress than I thought if you never realised it, but I've had plenty of time to think about why it didn't work. I think we were both too self-absorbed—you with your career, and me with playing a grown-up version of house.'

Lorinda looked from one to the other in astonishment. 'Then ... then it wasn't because Rick was in show business?'

Arna laughed lightly. 'Of course not! He could have been a car salesman or carpenter, for all the difference it would have made. What a man does has nothing to do with what he is.'

How could she have been so wrong? All these years she had taken it for granted that Rick's career as an entertainer was somehow to blame for his character flaws. She had believed that if only he'd had a steady nine-to-five job like other fathers, everything would have been different.

'You look a bit stunned, Anni-Lori. Are you feeling all right?'

'Yes, Rick, I'm ... I'm fine. Just tired, that's all. Would you mind if I left you two alone and had an early night?'

Their answering smiles assured her they would appreciate some time alone together to try to heal the breach of twelve years apart. They wished her goodnight and she fled to the sanctuary of her own room.

The truth was, she wasn't fine at all. In one night, the entire fabric of her life had been torn asunder and rewoven into a design she hardly recognised. More than anything, she needed time to think. Somehow she had made a ghastly mistake, and it had cost her Race's love—and perhaps the only true happiness she would ever know.

'What a man does has nothing to do with what he is' ... the thought echoed and re-echoed around her confused brain. Because she had always blamed her father's career for his weaknesses she had assumed that Race, having the same career, would be just as weak. Afraid that he would leave her as Rick had left Arna, she had spurned his love before he could have the chance to spurn her. She had driven him into Simone's all-too-willing arms and, remembering the dance's expression of triumph this morning, she knew Simone would make the most of her advantage.

With limbs that felt as if they were made of lead she undressed and slipped into a nightgown, then sat at her dressing table to begin her ritual hairbrushing.

But even this activity failed to have its usual soothing effort. With each brush stroke, she was tormented by visions of Race until the brush became his hands, stroking the hair back from her forehead after he saved her from the snake. A tremor shook her as she recalled how childishly embarrassed she had been that he had found her naked, but contrarily, the tender nerve endings of her skin throbbed with remembered sensations as she also recalled how close she had come to giving in to him that night. She thought of the feeling like hunger she had experienced as his questing fingers roved over her body under her terry-towelling gown. She had been a little mad, she thought now, inflamed by his touch until she was beyond reason. It would have been achingly easy to let him make love to her.

Instead she had rejected him out of the fear that he wouldn't remain faithful to her. The thought was like a dash of cold water over her as she recalled how she had pretended not to care about him and encouraged his belief that she was searching for a father substitute.

She believed then that she was doing the best thing for them both, so sure had she been that relationships were by their nature impermanent. Yet that was not borne out by the scene taking place in this flat, not a dozen feet from her bedroom door. Now she understood why Arna had never taken another lover or even sought a divorce from Rick. 'A day of marriage to him is worth a lifetime with someone else,' she had said. Was she right? *Was* it better to have loved and lost? She had been so busy avoiding emotional ties because she was afraid they wouldn't last that she had never given herself a chance to love or to lose. Arna had taken that chance, she saw now, and although it brought her some measure of heartache, it also brought enough happiness to sustain her for the last twelve years. Who knew what joy lay ahead of her now if only she and Rick could resolve their differences!

Lorinda had been an utter fool, she admitted it now. By judging Race on evidence she now knew to be false she had driven him away. Tears sprang to her eyes as she envisaged him with Simone. The last show would be over by now and they would be strolling back to their suites—or more likely, to Simone's suite—in the moonlight and balmy warmth of the island night.

The gypsy was right. As a tall dark stranger he had come into her life and had, indeed, taken something from her. Despite her best efforts to prevent it, he had taken her heart and left behind an empty shell which answered to the name of Lorinda Fleming.

CHAPTER TEN

'You look like you need a holiday to recover from your holiday, Lori,' Marla told her when she arrived at the office next morning.

'I wasn't exactly on holiday, you know.'

Her friend grinned. 'Oh no? All that slaving over a hot beach and looking decorative around a pool wore you out, did it? Or is it the strain of being engaged to a gorgeous hunk like Race Wolfendale?' Her eye went automatically to Lorinda's left hand and she gasped involuntarily. 'Oh-oh! We pause for a station break while Marla McGovern takes her foot out of her mouth!'

Lorinda hugged her reassuringly. 'It's O.K., you couldn't have known the engagement was off. I only told Max last night.'

'Oh, Lori, what happened?'

'That's just it—nothing. We shouldn't have become engaged in the first place. I suppose we mistook a casual romance for the real thing.'

Marla let her breath out slowly. 'But you *are* in love with him, though.'

Lorinda shot her a startled glance. 'Does it show that much?'

'It's not written on your forehead or anything,' Marla said with unconvincing lightness. 'It's more a sort of haunted look in your eyes that wasn't there before you went to Windi Bay.'

Haunted? Strangely enough that was precisely how she felt. She should have known Marla would spot it. After five years of sharing work and play they knew each other almost as well as sisters. 'Do me a favour?' she asked.

'Name it.'

'Don't say anything to Max. He'll only blame himself, and it wasn't his fault.'

As Marla nodded agreement, another voice spoke behind them. 'What wasn't his fault?'

Lorinda jumped, 'Hello, Max, I didn't hear you come in.'

'If you were talking about Simone's mishap, I've already spoken on the phone to Gerhardt Muller and assured him that nobody's blaming Windi Bay. Simone is in hospital in Cairns and she confirmed it was her own fault, although she won't give me any details of exactly how she came to hurt her ankle.'

'In hospital? But she told me her ankle was only twisted. If I'd known it was serious I would have stayed at the resort.'

'You weren't to know,' Max assured her. 'Apparently she told everyone the same thing. She managed to do the closing show, but afterwards it seems she was in such pain that they had to fly her to the mainland for treatment. It sounds like more than a twisted ankle to me, don't you agree?'

'It sure does.' She wondered whether she should tell him about Simone's odd behaviour before she twisted her ankle, if that was in fact what was wrong. She decided there was no point in bringing it up unless the dancer decided to sue the resort, which didn't seem likely.

Max's next comment confirmed this assumption. 'Simone's contract with us is ended, so, as the lady ungraciously pointed out, what she does now is none of our business. But just as a precaution, I wired her manager in Honolulu to tell him what happened.'

'Is ... is Race staying in Cairns with Simone?'

Lorinda asked hesitantly, aware that her voice sounded husky with emotion.

Max studied her curiously. 'No, of course not. He flew to Adelaide for the Festival Centre concert, then he's due in Sydney to appear on the Dick Elder show at the end of the week. Of course, he could decide to see Simone after that, but that's his affair.'

Race would be back in Sydney in another two days. The thought sent twin jolts of pleasure and pain shooting through her. Pleasure because she would have a few more precious hours to be near him and pain because Max was probably right. As soon as he had fulfilled his contract, Race would probably fly back to Cairns to Simone's side. Perhaps it would be better if she didn't see him at all. She wasn't sure she could bear the pain of another parting, especially now she knew how badly she had misjudged him.

She closed her eyes against the anguish this thought brought with it, but opened them again when Max spoke to her. 'Come into my office, Lorinda. I want to discuss the Westsiders' tour with you, since you'll be handling most of the arrangements.'

Like a robot, she followed him into the glass-walled office and he shut the door, indicating that she should take a chair. Nervously she perched on the edge of the seat.

Max looked back to where Marla was seated at her reception desk. She was looking curiously their way, but turned back to her work when Max caught her eye. A moment later, the furious tapping of typewriter keys reached them through the closed door.

'I was hoping we'd get this chance to talk,' he said.

'About the Westsiders?'

'In a minute. First it's you I'm worried about. What happened between you and Race Wolfendale?' She blushed scarlet and he frowned. 'Not the personal details, of course. I mean the on-again-off-again engagement.'

'There's very little to tell,' she said simply, deciding that it was better to be honest with him this time. 'Simone was being a nuisance, so Race told her we were engaged to ensure that she left me in peace.'

'And it backfired when she went to the press? That little shrew! But why didn't you tell me that when I rang to congratulate you?'

'I couldn't, Max.' She went on to tell him of her concern for her mother.

'I see,' he said gravely. 'So you're still heartwhole, is that what you're trying to say?'

How could she tell him that she would never be heartwhole again? He was bound to blame himself for sending her to Windi Bay with Race, and she couldn't hurt him like that. Besides, there was nothing he could do to help. 'Please, I'd rather not discuss it any more,' she told him, and prayed that he would respect her wish.

To her relief, he did, and turned the conversation to her father's return. 'How did Arna take it?'

'She was thrilled beyond words. I didn't realise how much she still loved Rick, in spite of everything.'

'Neither did I.' Max replied sharply. It was Lorinda's turn to look at him in wonder. Could Max be in love with Arna? It seemed so plain now that she wondered how she had missed it for so long. Poor Max! He must have been hoping Arna would agree to marry him one day, and now Rick had returned and ruined everything.

'I'm so sorry, Max,' she said softly.

His eyes misted over and he squeezed her hand affectionately. 'Seems we all have our problems, don't we?' He cleared his throat noisily and moved around to sit at his desk then drew a sheaf of papers towards him. 'Let's get on with this. We have to prepare a complete press kit on the Westsiders in time for their arrival on Thursday afternoon. They record a special at A.T.C. on Friday, but I'll take care of that. All the information you need for the press releases and so on is in this folder.' He pushed a glossy photo across the desk to her. 'That's Allan West, the band leader. Twenty-eight, single and devastatingly charming, by all accounts.'

In his own gruff way, Max was trying to tell her there were other fish in the sea besides Race Wolfendale. She studied the photo and agreed with Max that Allan West was extremely good-looking, but he wasn't Race, and she knew now that all the love she was capable of giving belonged only to him. Something died inside her when she walked away from him and she felt so cold and empty now that she doubted whether it was within her power ever to love again. But there was no point in hurting Max by telling him how she felt, so she obliged him by making approving noises over the photo.

He beamed encouragingly. 'That's the spirit! Off to work now. I don't want to hear from you again until that press kit is ready.'

She gave him a mock salute. 'Aye, aye, sir!' With the folder under her arm she returned to her own desk.

She became so absorbed in preparing biographies of the band members and their leader and drafting a press release about their tour that she was oblivious of the time slipping past until Marla appeared at her elbow.

'Have you given up eating after Windi Bay, or are you joining me for some lunch?'

It was on the tip of her tongue to say she wasn't hungry and suggest that Marla go off by herself, but

the secretary looked so appealingly at her that she
relented and closed the file decisively. 'Diet lunch or
The Works?'

Marla cocked her head to one side. 'It's your first
day back so let's celebrate at The Works.'

Diet lunch usually meant a wholemeal sandwich and
fruit lunch eaten in the park near their office, but
occasionally they treated themselves to a sit-down
lunch at The Works, a small café in the nearby
shopping complex. Today they were lucky to obtain
one of the café's balcony tables where they could
overlook the shopping crowds. A waitress took their
orders for toasted club sandwiches and coffee and they
sat back to watch the passing parade.

'Do you realise this is where the whole thing
began?' Marla asked.

'What whole thing?'

'The gypsy fortune-teller. Her tent was down there
in the fountain court beside those potted palms. Oh
look, she's still here!'

Lorinda followed Marla's pointing finger and
stiffened as her eye rested on the garishly coloured
tent still set up in the courtyard. If it hadn't been for
the gypsy and her warning about tall dark strangers,
she might have been more receptive to Race when he
first invited her out—and just maybe, she might have
avoided making such a terrible mistake about him.

Noticing her pale face, Marla patted her arm.
'Relax, Lori. I'm sure all those things about your
mother getting sick and the inheritance and all were
just coincidences.'

'You're probably right. I'm just being silly,'
Lorinda agreed, and tried to relax. Still, she knew she
would never wholly believe they were coincidences,
whatever Marla thought. She turned her attention to
the plates of food which were set in front of them, but

found it almost impossible to concentrate on Marla's cheerful description of life at the office while she had been away. She felt tense and irritable, with a terrible sense of foreboding.

'Well, well—we meet again!'

The balcony lurched around her as she looked up into the flashing dark eyes of the gypsy woman. 'It's you,' she whispered. Where had the woman appeared from?

'Yes, it is I. And I see from your face that everything I foretold came to pass—did it not?'

Lorinda looked away and heard the gypsy laugh harshly. 'Your curse about the tall dark stranger was accurate enough,' she said almost inaudibly.

'Curse? Oh, I didn't say it was a curse, only that it would come to pass.' She looked keenly at Lorinda. 'Whether it is good or bad for you is up to yourself.'

'Oh, come along, Elsie, our lunch break is nearly over!' They watched in astonishment as another woman in a ragged print dress with curlers in her hair tugged at the 'gypsy's' arm. Muttering, the gypsy—if that was what she was—followed her companion to the lunch counter.

Marla suppressed a giggle. 'You see? She's no more of a gypsy than I am, so you can stop worrying.'

Still, gypsy or not, Lorinda was disturbed by the woman's comments. It was true, she hadn't said her prediction was a warning, now she came to think about it, but Lorinda had taken it as such. Was she wrong about that, too, as she had been wrong about almost everything to do with Race Wolfendale? Listlessly she pushed her plate away.

'You've hardly eaten a thing,' protested Marla. 'You could have caught something on that island. Maybe you should see a doctor.'

She could have told Marla that no doctor could cure

what she had 'caught' on Windi Bay. She was afflicted with a hopeless case of love for a man who despised her because of a supposed father fixation. What did it matter if the gypsy's message was a blessing or a curse? It was too late anyway. She had succeeded in driving Race into the arms of Simone Dyson and nothing she could do now would change things.

Max was talking on the phone when they returned to the office. He replaced the receiver and looked up as Lorinda walked in. 'That was Tony Presley calling from Honolulu.'

'Simone's manager?'

'That's right. It seems I did the right thing by contacting him. He sounded very anxious and wanted to know the quickest way to get to Cairns. There must be more than a business relationship between them to make him come haring over here from Hawaii like that.'

Lorinda's heart went out to the stranger as she thought of the disappointment that lay in store for him when he reached Cairns and found Simone wearing Race Wolfendale's ring.

The black mood this thought brought on persisted throughout the afternoon and was still with her when she arrived home that evening. A note in her mother's handwriting was propped up against a flower vase in the centre of the dining table. 'Hope you had a good day, darling. Rick and I have gone out to catch up on old times. Don't wait up for us. Love, Mum.'

In the silence of the small flat she could hear her heart pounding deafeningly loud and she felt a pressing ache start up behind her eyes. She knew that Rick had spent the night at the flat, because this morning his suitcase was still where she left it under the table. The door to her mother's bedroom had been closed, so rather than intrude, she had rustled up some breakfast for herself and left for work as quietly as possible.

She didn't begrudge Arna her new-found happiness, she felt sure. Heaven knew, she deserved some joy after the hard years that lay behind her. No, she was pleased for them both that the reunion appeared to be a success. So why did she have this overwhelming feeling of loneliness?

Then she faced the fact that she was jealous of Rick and Arna because they possessed what she would have given her soul to own—true love. 'Unconditional', Arna called it. It was all Race had asked of her, and she had turned him away for reasons which now seemed foolish beyond belief. She had told herself it was because of the heart-wrenching partings she had experienced as a child and the misery her mother endured after Rick left. But the real reason, she saw now with blinding clarity, was fear. As a child she had blamed herself for driving her father away. Now, she still feared she was unworthy of love—but this time she had *really* driven Race away.

Overcome with unhappiness, she sank down on to a chair and buried her face in her hands. When they had first met she told Race she didn't need him probing into her mind. But she did, she did! It was so clear now that she marvelled it had taken her so long to see it. Race had known it from the moment they met, but she did not want to be convinced and rejected his persistent attempts to reach her just so the child in her could say, 'I told you so.'

But what about Simone? *Could* she have competed with the exotic beauty and charisma of Race's former wife? Even an hour ago she would have said no, but she wasn't going to be led down that same path again. Race could have been hers—he had only returned to Simone because Lorinda had forced him to.

She found some measure of comfort in the thought, although she knew it wasn't going to help her through the long, lonely years that stretched ahead. For no one could take his place. Gerhardt had been very perceptive when he said he could not compete with the talents and personality of Race Wolfendale. No man could. Still, no matter what the future held or didn't hold, she could cling to the knowledge that he had cared for her once. For a heady moment she wished she *had* let him make love to her in her room at Windi Bay, so she would have the ultimate memory of him.

Then she gave herself a mental shake. There was no point in mooning over what she had lost. The sooner she started facing the future without Race, the better.

Facing the future was easier said than done, she discovered, especially when one worked for a casting agency. She seemed fated to open an actors' register and find Race's features staring at her from a glossy ten-by-eight photo, or to come across his name in the files when she was looking for something else. She told herself it was just bad luck, but wondered, all the same, if her hands were telling her what her brain would not—that she *was* hungry for news of him, however much she tried to deny it.

Fortunately the next two days were hectic ones as she prepared for the concert tour to be given by the Westsiders. The English jazz band was enormously popular and their concerts were booked out well in advance. Their television special was also eagerly awaited by their fans.

'The studio has been besieged by people wanting to be in the audience for the taping,' she told Allan West as they travelled by limousine to the studios of Australian Television Corporation, known in the business as A.T.C.

The bandleader grinned. 'That's what I like to hear! You and Max did a great job of arranging everything.'

'Thank you, Mr West.'

'When are you going to drop this Mister business and call me Allan?' he chided. 'After all, you are having dinner with me tonight.'

Lorinda stared at him in astonishment. 'I am not! I told you, Mr West ... er ... I mean Allan ...'

'I know,' he sighed, 'you prefer to keep things strictly business. Well, you can't blame a man for trying.'

She was sorry she couldn't be more encouraging, because she genuinely liked Allan West. As well as being good-looking he possessed a warm, likeable personality and she had the feeling he would be good company. But with Race still constantly in her thoughts, it wouldn't be fair to go out with someone else. Perhaps later when she had adjusted to the idea of a life without him, she might start dating again, but not now; it was too soon.

The other members of the band were setting up their equipment by the time she and Allan walked into the A.T.C. studios. Allan's arrival was greeted by a chorus of shrieks from the audience gathered to watch the taping. Allan waved to them and strode across to join his band while Lorinda chatted to the floor manager. He told her they were taping a production number and she knew this meant the band would be working with a team of dancers and some spectacular special effects.

'It looks glamorous on screen, but it's all hard work at this end—since we have to run through the entire number without a break,' he told her. Lorinda nodded sympathetically.

She declined his invitation to watch from the master control room located high above the studio floor, preferring to take an inconspicuous seat on the fringe of the audience. The discordant noises from the studio floor told her the band was tuning up. At a signal from the floor manager, an 'Applause' sign lit up and the audience clapped furiously in response. Then the band swung into a lively tune which she recognised as one of Allan West's own compositions. Almost of its own accord her foot began to tap in time to the music and she relaxed for the first time in days.

Without warning, they went straight into the opening bars of 'The Night, the Stars and You.' It was a jazz rendition, but she would have recognised the song anywhere because it was engraved forever on her heart and mind. She had an urge to flee from the studio to escape the flood of tender memories the music evoked, but because the videotape was running, she couldn't move without ruining the take. Emotionally over-wrought as she was, she was enough of a professional to stay in her seat until the 'Applause' sign came on again, signalling the end of the number. Allan West came over to her at once, and she could see the audience regarding her with curiosity and some envy.

'Well, what did you think of that?' he asked, mopping his forehead, which was damp from the heat of the studio lighting.

'It was very good,' she said a little stiffly.

He pouted slightly. 'You didn't like it! I thought the medley was rather a nice touch—my own arrangement.'

'It was,' she said, trying to put conviction into her voice. 'That last tune ... brought back a few memories, that's all.'

'Something you'd prefer to forget?'

'Something I have to learn to live with,' she said firmly, and got to her feet. 'Excuse me, Allan. I think I'll go and get some coffee at the Summer Camp.'

She left him staring after her in puzzlement, but didn't feel up to explaining herself any further to him. The Summer Camp was the in-house nickname for the canteen used by studio personnel and visitors. As usual, it was a hive of activity and her arrival attracted no attention at all, for which she was grateful.

At the self-service counter, she collected coffee and a Danish pastry which she carried to a corner table. She hoped no one would ask to sit with her, because she didn't feel like talking to anyone right now. Her wish was granted and she sipped her coffee slowly while she recovered from the shock of hearing Race's song again. She should have expected it since he had made it an international hit, but that didn't make it any easier to endure. Damn Race Wolfendale! Was she to be haunted by reminders of him everywhere she went?

As if in response to her thoughts, a figure darkened the entrance to the canteen. It was Race! Then Lorinda remembered that he was guest starring on the Dick Elder Show, being recorded in another studio on the same lot. Max must have known he'd be here today—that was why he had insisted she go in his place at the last moment. She had wondered about the change in plans but believed Max when he said he had another appointment he couldn't postpone. She had no reason not to believe him, or to suspect that he was scheming to get her and Race together again. Max probably didn't know that Race and Simone had once been married or that they had become reconciled at Windi Bay.

She must get out of here before Race saw her, but how? There was only one entrance, and he was blocking it as he scanned the crowd of diners, many of whom were still in costume as they snatched a bite of lunch during a break in filming.

A copy of *Variety* lay on a chair beside her, probably left behind by another diner and she snatched it up thankfully. But before she could hide behind the page and pretend to be reading it, there was a voice at her side.

'Hello, Lorinda.'

She looked up into eyes that seemed if possible more fiery than she remembered. His week in the tropics had deepened his tan to a rich mahogany which contrasted with the snowy whiteness of his dress shirt. It was unbuttoned almost to the waist and his tie hung at half-mast as if he had wrenched it loose as soon as the cameras stopped turning. Distractedly, she noticed how his wiry black chest hair curled around the edges of his shirt as if seeking escape from the confines of his clothes.

'Well, aren't you going to say something?'

She became aware that she was staring at him. 'Hello, Race,' she said tightly. 'You'll have to excuse me, I'm needed in Studio A.' Before he could react she pushed past him and half ran out of the canteen.

'Lorinda, wait!'

She didn't look back, but the sound of footsteps on the polished floor told her he was following her. 'Go away!' she choked. The sight of him so soon after hearing the band play his song was more than her shattered nerves could endure, and the tears began to rain down her cheeks. Blinded, she turned into the first doorway she came to and leaned against it, hoping he would walk on. But he followed her into the room and snapped on a light. At once she turned away before he could see her tears, then screamed as she came hard up against a full-grown grizzly bear rearing up on its hind legs. She stepped backwards and Race caught her as she stumbled, turning her around to face him.

'It's all right, it's not real,' he soothed. Looking nervously around, she saw that he was right. She had blundered into a prop room and the bear was a fibreglass replica from some long-forgotten TV show. It was surrounded by masses of papier-mâché flowers, polystyrene boulders, a miniature space ship and an odd assortment of period furniture.

'I'm all right—I was startled, that's all,' she said, but Race continued to hold her against his chest. The breath caught in her throat at the feel of his hard, muscular body against hers.

Gently he smoothed the hair back from her forehead. 'When are you going to stop running away?' he asked. She began to protest, but he shushed her. 'I know all about Rick Brennan.'

She looked up at him in wonder. 'How did you find out?'

'Gerhardt Muller told me. When he realised I'd let you go without a struggle, he called me all kinds of a fool. He was right. You should have told me Rick was your father.'

'Would it have made any difference?'

'The hell it would! I thought you couldn't get over this father fixation you let me believe you had, so when I saw you with Rick I thought ... well, Gerhardt was right, I behaved like a fool.'

'Without a struggle? I don't understand. You and Simone ... I thought ...'

'You thought we were lovers. I know. You wouldn't let me explain that I went there to threaten her with murder if she pulled any more fool stunts like leaving that snake in your room.'

Lorinda's head was spinning with the unexpectedness of what she was hearing. 'Then you were only protecting me? But you and Simone *were* married once?'

'Yes, but it was a long time ago. Let me tell you about it.' Gently, he drew her down beside him on to a velvet-upholstered chaise-longue. 'When I started out in show business, it was a long hard fight to the top, singing in sleazy night spots for pennies . . . that sort of thing. I vowed I would never marry until I could give my wife a secure existence. Later, when I made it to the top, I was still travelling too much to offer a girl anything more than financial security, so I stayed single. I was no monk, don't get me wrong, but there were no permanent attachments, because I wouldn't allow myself to get involved with anyone.'

'But you married Simone.'

'I was getting sick of my own company. She and I got along well and I figured since we were in the same business, she knew the score and wouldn't expect a cottage with roses around the door.'

'But it didn't turn out the way you planned, did it?'

He shaded his eyes with one hand as he coped with an unhappy memory. 'No, it didn't. We were married one morning, then the same afternoon I overheard her on the phone gloating to a friend how she planned to swindle me out of half of everything I owned under California's community property laws.'

Lorinda drew a sharp breath. She had never suspected anything like this. 'I'm so sorry, Race,' she breathed.

'Don't be—I'm not. It was just luck that I found out in time. I didn't even stop to pack, I just walked out and had the marriage annulled before the ink was dry on the certificate.'

'When you never said anything, I thought . . .'

'You thought I was protecting my image.'

'But it was really Simone you were protecting, wasn't it?'

'That's right. If word got around that she was a

crook, her career would have been finished. As it is, she's getting her retribution after all.'

'I don't understand,' said Lorinda. 'What do you mean?'

'She has an incurable bone disease which will end her dancing career. She shouldn't have taken the Windi Bay job because she was in no shape to handle it, but she saw it as a chance to persuade me to take her back.'

So that explained Simone's curious behaviour on the beach when Lorinda glimpsed an expression of pain on her face. She was ill, but had been pretending that all was well, hoping to lure Race into remarrying her to replace her shattered career. 'What will she do now?' she asked.

'That's Tony Presley's problem. As well as being her manager he's wanted to marry her for years, but she's always turned him down, although she had a child by him years ago. It might be the best thing for all of them if they got together as a family.'

So the child of the rumours didn't belong to Race either! A thought occurred to Lorinda that sent tremors of excitement surging through her. 'Race, why are you telling me all this?' she asked.

'Because I've been in love with you since the day I set eyes on you. I vowed never to let any woman affect me this way, but you're driving me crazy. Tell me you'll marry me, for Pete's sake!'

'Oh yes, Race!' she breathed, and all the love she had worked so hard to conceal came shining out of her eyes.

He gave a huge sigh of relief. 'Thank goodness! I was so afraid you didn't feel the same way as I did, even after I found out why you kept running away from me.'

'How did you find that out?'

He smiled knowingly. 'I had a long talk with Rick and Arna this morning after you left for work. They helped me to understand why you reacted towards me the way you did.' His expression grew serious. 'Lori, I live my life in the glare of the spotlight anywhere between London, L.A., Vegas, Monte Carlo . . . my Santa Barbara house can be our base if it's any help, but you'll never have a nine-to-five existence with me, and I still can't give you a cottage with roses around the door, at least not to live in permanently.'

Lorinda lifted a hand and traced the firm outline of his jaw then put a finger to his lips to silence him. 'It's all right. I used to think those things were important, but I've learned a lot since I came back to Sydney. Seeing my parents get back together helped me to get a few things straight in my own mind. I don't need roses around the door any more. All I need is you.' For a fleeting moment she was tempted to tell him about the gypsy and her prediction, but she decided there was plenty of time for that. Besides, how could he take anything of value from her when everything she had she would give to him willingly from this day forward?

Race seemed to sense the direction her thoughts were taking, because he bent his dark head to hers and kissed her with all the passion she had imagined in her dreams. Ardently, she responded, and the kiss went on for a long time before he drew away from her reluctantly, to reach into his jacket and bring out a white jeweller's case.

This time, when he placed the engagement ring on her finger she knew it was there to stay, as a symbol of the wealth of love which existed between them.

'Remember what I said to you in another guise?' he asked, and she had a momentary vision of him made up as the Shakespearean actor, 'David Hewitt'.

'I remember,' she said, suddenly shy. 'But tell me again anyway.'

' "Doubt that the stars are fire, Doubt that the sun doth move, Doubt truth to be a liar, But never doubt I love",' he quoted.

Her eyes were moist, but with tears of pure happiness this time. 'I'll never doubt it again as long as I live,' she vowed before his mouth came down to claim hers again.

THE ORIGIN OF THE GYPSIES

Lorinda's Gypsy fortune-teller belongs to one of the most misunderstood cultures in the world. A nomadic people, Gypsies were banished from one country after another because of their odd customs and language. Enterprising and resilient, they made homes wherever they landed.

It is believed that Gypsies were expelled from India by the Mongol warrior Tamerlane in the fifteenth century. Dispersed into Europe, the chiefs of the three main wandering tribes—the Kalderosh, the Gitanos and the Manushes—facetiously called themselves the "dukes of little Egypt," from which the name Gypsy derives. Each tribe had strict political and moral codes; if one of these was breached, the wrongdoer was exiled, for to remain would pollute the entire society. Many of those exiled joined sedentary Gypsy groups and set up housekeeping. One such community, near Granada, Spain, lives in caves with electricity and carpeting.

Though the men have traditionally been undertakers in Rumania, musicians in Spain and hop pickers in England, women have been the steadier breadwinners, earning money as fortune-tellers, entertainers and beggars. Along with keeping the earnings in a common fund, women have also been the guardians of the moral code. While Gypsies refer to themselves by the name *rom,* meaning man, and their language is called Romany, it is really the women who have the upper hand!

Once persecuted in many European countries for witchcraft and often made scapegoats for crimes committed by others—in the nineteenth century many such were sent to the penal colonies of Australia—Gypsies have found more tolerance in today's world. We have benefited from their colorful music and other forms of entertainment, such as tarot-card reading—but strangely there is little literature. This is because Gypsies have always been reluctant to reveal their inner world; which explains, perhaps, why their language is not a written one. To most outsiders they are an unusual people—to some, fascinating. And chances are the origins and customs of Gypsies will remain shrouded in mystery, intriguing people everywhere for years to come.